WEAR

B MIL

P|
Yo
n
or
P|

(

D1387764

DARROW'S GAMBLE

'Set a thief to catch a thief!' It's a risky strategy for a lawman to take, but Sheriff Darrow has very personal reasons for wanting to catch bank robber Tom Croucher. Forced to stay in Wyoming, Darrow is relying on two convicted criminals, Tomcat Billy and Irish, to do the job for him. But Tomcat hates Darrow, while Irish wants to go straight. They join Croucher's gang, but who deserves their loyalty — the outlaw or the sheriff?

GILLIAN F. TAYLOR

DARROW'S GAMBLE

Complete and Unabridged

LINFORD
Leicester

First published in Great Britain in 2013 by
Robert Hale Limited
London

First Linford Edition
published 2015
by arrangement with
Robert Hale Limited
London

A catalogue record for this book is available
from the British Library.

ISBN 978–1–4448–2538–1

Published by
F. A. Thorpe (Publishing)
Anstey, Leicestershire

Set by Words & Graphics Ltd.
Anstey, Leicestershire
Printed and bound in Great Britain by
T. J. International Ltd., Padstow, Cornwall

This book is printed on acid-free paper

1

Sheriff Beauchief Darrow paused outside the drugstore to read his deputy's elegant, if rather illegible, handwriting. When he finished the letter he smiled suddenly, transforming his usually stern face. Folding the letter, he continued briskly along Main Street, Govan. The Wyoming railroad town was thriving, thanks in good part to the sheriff's own work, and the streets were busy on this fine October afternoon.

Darrow waited for a wagon loaded with beer barrels to pass before he made his way over the junction of Cross Street and Main Street. On the corner was the town's funeral parlour, the undertaker himself sitting in a rocking chair on the sidewalk. Darrow stopped beside him, but Josh Turnage took no notice, continuing to read the playscript he was holding.

'I guess your customers don't mind waiting some while you learn your lines,' Darrow remarked, in the rich drawl of a Southern aristocrat.

'The dead ones don't, but their dearly beloved can get nasty iffen I take too long over the burying,' Turnage replied, looking up at last.

The undertaker was a lean man, often unnervingly intense but sometimes unnervingly outgoing. The intensity was enhanced by a villainous moustache, waxed and curled at the ends, grown for his role as the wicked squire in the Amateur Players' last melodrama, which had been a big hit a month ago.

'I don't suppose you're doing Shakespeare next?' Darrow asked. Unlike Turnage, who had sawdust caught in his rolled-up sleeves, the sheriff was, as always, tidily dressed. The only touch of colour in his black, grey and white clothing was a blue silk bandanna worn as a cravat. He carried himself well, and in spite of his gunbelt and sheriff's badge, no one would mistake him for anything but a gentleman.

Turnage gave a sudden, shark-like smile. 'I'm afraid it's The Murder in the Red Barn this time.'

'That sounds like Hugh's level of sophistication,' Darrow drawled. He held up the folded letter. 'He may even be back in time to see it. I just picked up this letter from him. Hugh and Minnie are already on their way back from Europe and should be back in Govan by early November.'

Darrow's chief deputy, Hugh Keating, was an Englishman, the second son of a baronet, sent abroad by his family for reasons that varied whenever he was asked. Life in Govan, and his relationship with Minnie, had settled him down. Although he planned to live here in Govan with his American wife, they had gone to Europe for their extended honeymoon following their wedding that summer.

'I thought they planned to spend the winter in Italy instead of freezing to death out here?' Turnage replied.

'A sudden change of circumstances.'

Darrow smiled. 'Minnie is expecting.'

'Well, that was quick work.'

Darrow nodded. 'The baby is due in April. They wish to be back in Govan for the birth, and don't want to be sailing the Atlantic in the winter, so Hugh has been unusually decisive, and arranged for them to return at once.'

Turnage grinned. 'He was probably missing having you shout at him.'

'Probably.' Always alert, Darrow turned his attention further along the street.

His gaze settled on four horses hitched in front of the next building, which was the First Govan Bank. They were well-made animals, carrying bed-rolls and saddle-bags. They could have been cowhands' go-to-town horses, but Darrow knew that today wasn't payday for any of the local ranches, and the nearest horse, the one he could see best, didn't have a rope on its saddle. It did have an empty rifle scabbard though. Alert now, Darrow scanned more of the street, keeping his movement casual.

A little further away, on the other side of the street, a mounted man was waiting outside the livery barn. He was watching the comings and goings on Main Street, with particular attention to the bank, and had his hand resting near the butt of his pistol.

'What is it?' Turnage asked, seeing the sudden tension in the sheriff.

'Got your shotgun handy?' Darrow asked quietly, turning slightly so his crescent-and-star badge was not obvious to the man waiting across the street.

'In the workshop.' Turnage closed the playscript and put it down.

'Go and get it; the bank's being robbed.'

Turnage made no fuss, simply rose and walked steadily into his undertaker's shop. Darrow beckoned sharply to a dishevelled man leaning against the corner of the building. 'Edison.'

The drunk looked round, blinked, smiled, and peeled himself away from the building to approach the sheriff.

'What kin I be doin' for you?' Edison enquired amiably.

Darrow spoke urgently. 'Don't make a fuss.' He paused, making sure that Edison understood. 'Go to my office and tell Deputy Pacey that the bank's being robbed. Tell him to bring shotguns and approach cautiously.'

Edison nodded, continuing the gesture slightly too long, then turned and shambled across the street. Darrow's mouth narrowed in distaste, then he dismissed the drunk from his mind. A quick glance into the undertaker's drew a blank: Turnage was still fetching his shotgun from his workshop out back. Darrow was glancing back down the street towards his office when the bank's door opened.

Four armed men came out in a bunch, the last one moving sideways to keep his gun pointed at the people inside the building. All were carrying bulky burlap sacks tied up at the neck. Sheriff Darrow had his gun drawn and aimed before the first one, a tallish man with thick black hair, could step off the sidewalk.

'Hold it!' The sheriff commanded. 'Surrender!'

The four bandits whipped round, barely twenty feet from where the sheriff stood.

Darrow fired first, loosing two shots before leaping off the sidewalk. A cry of pain told him he'd made one hit at least. Darrow's view of the bandits was blocked by a frightened bay horse hitched out front of the undertaker's. He bent slightly, using the animal as cover while he assessed the situation. The bandits were mounting but as the sheriff tried to aim his gun, the horse he was standing beside cow-kicked, almost catching him with a hind hoof. A bandit with thick red hair fired in Darrow's direction. The bay squealed and swung about, almost barging Darrow off his feet.

The sheriff cursed and moved out into the street, hoping for a clearer shot. The bandits were turning their horses, urging them into a gallop. Wagons and drays had halted as drivers abandoned their high seats for safer spots. Pedestrians were ducking into shops and taking whatever shelter they could find. The four riders spurred their horses away, but Darrow could see that one was sitting awkwardly in his saddle, one hand pressed against his leg. As the sheriff raised his Colt, he realized there was one other person moving on the street. The lookout was riding towards him, gun aimed.

Darrow dived back for the dubious shelter of the agitated bay. A bullet zipped past him and crashed through the window of the funeral parlour. Darrow ducked and turned back, aware that the other bandits were escaping while he fought this one.

'God damn you!' yelled Turnage, who had just appeared in the door of his shop. He fired his shotgun over Darrow's head. 'That glass is expensive!'

The bandit screamed in pain. His

horse bucked, throwing him from the saddle, then bolted along Main Street. Darrow saw he'd dropped his gun, and glimpsed Turnage moving across the sidewalk. Trusting the other man to cover the injured bandit, Darrow sprinted back into the centre of the street. The other bank robbers were fleeing, not bothering to try and shoot. Raising his Colt with both hands, Darrow aimed at the centre of the group and fired.

One man, the one he'd already hit, jerked and then slid sideways from his racing horse. He crumpled into the dirt of the street, limp before he'd even hit the ground. The black-haired man hauled on his reins, bringing his horse to a dirt-skidding stop.

'Dan!'

He turned his horse, but a big, bulky bandit had also halted, and grabbed his arm.

Darrow fired again, missing this time. He was uncomfortably aware that there were still people on the street, and a missed shot could kill a bystander as easily as its intended target.

'Surrender!' Darrow shouted.

The black-haired man had been leaning from his saddle, looking at the one Darrow had shot. His big companion said something the sheriff didn't hear. The bandit looked in Darrow's direction, then abruptly swung his horse around and spurred it into a gallop again, the other man alongside him.

Darrow sprinted after them but a lumber wagon prevented him from getting another clear shot. As he reached the one who'd fallen, the riders turned sharply between buildings, vanishing from his sight as they headed for the edge of town. Halting, Darrow spun and saw Turnage had control of the injured lookout, while Deputy Pacey was sprinting towards him, holding a shotgun. A few paces behind him was Deputy Maloney, hired temporarily through Hugh's absence. Satisfied that the immediate situation was under control, the sheriff knelt to examine the man lying in the street. There was a neat bullet hole in the back of his jacket collar, but no blood. The bullet had smashed through his spine at the back of his neck, killing him almost instantly. Darrow rose and turned abruptly to face his regular deputy.

'Get our horses; Turnage will take care of things here.'

'You're leaving the undertaker in charge?' the tall, handsome deputy asked.

'He's not paid to risk his neck chasing outlaws. You and Maloney are. I want both of you with me on this. Josh can cope with sorting out the mess here.'

'This town needs more lawmen,' Pacey said as he turned towards the livery stable.

Darrow didn't answer, but went to give orders to Maloney and Turnage.

★   ★   ★

It had been dark over an hour when Josh Turnage finally heard the lawmen returning to their office. As the door opened, he got up and moved the coffee pot to the top of the stove. Darrow's sour expression told Josh that the chase had been unsuccessful.

'Did you find any sign of them?' he asked.

'Some,' Darrow answered. 'They were going south, surely heading for Colorado.'

'We ain't but sixty miles from the border,' Maloney remarked, dropping heavily into one of the office chairs.

'They're probably out of our jurisdiction already,' Pacey added, returning shotguns to the rack on the side wall of the office.

The welcome smell of hot coffee began to fill the air. Darrow removed his coat and hung it from a stand in the corner near the gun rack. The law office was a functional room, with a leather-topped desk, a safe and filing cabinet nearby, and a smaller table by the gun rack. It gained character from the contents of two shelves and a noticeboard by the door leading to the cells. The shelf behind the desk sported Darrow's leather-bound law books, battered copies of *Great Expectations* and *Bleak House*, and a tin of Arbuckle's coffee beans. The one on the rear wall held some dime novels piled atop one another, a tin printed with a garish tartan design and other odds and ends. The notice board was filled with official notices, Wanted posters and a faded shopping list in Hugh's handwriting that fluttered from one corner.

'I got Doc Travis in to pick pellets out of the one I put lead into,' Turnage told them. 'His name's Cotter; I figured he'd be best in one of the inside cells for now. I wired the law at Laramie about the robbery, and asked them to pass the information on. The feller you killed is back at my place; I reckon this is him.' Turnage handed a Wanted dodger to the sheriff.

'Dan Croucher,' Darrow read aloud.

Pacey came up behind him and read over his shoulder. 'Looks like you bagged yourself a four hundred dollar reward, Darrow.'

'Well now,' Darrow said, smiling darkly. 'That might almost be reward enough for listening to you talking all the time we were chasing the rest of them.'

'Dan Croucher won't be a loss to society,' Maloney remarked. The older man had eased off his boots, and sat with his legs stretched out. 'Ain't no one much 'cept his brother, Captain Tom, going to miss him.'

'*Captain* Tom?' Pacey queried, turning to face the other deputy. 'Likes to give himself an officer's rank, does he?' As he spoke, he drew himself up into a military stance.

Pacey was an imposing figure when he reverted to the military posture drummed into him during officer school. Just over six feet tall, he was athletic and good-looking, with curly brown hair. He was a good horseman

14

and a good shot, and had done well during his five-year stint with the cavalry. Chances of promotion were low, however, so he'd chosen not to sign up again, and had moved into law work.

Maloney, however, was too tired to be impressed. He performed a spine-cracking stretch then slumped down into his hard chair.

'The Crouchers, Tom and Dan, rode in one of those Missouri Rough Riders outfits during the war,' Maloney told them. 'Young and vicious they was, and when the war was done, they didn't figure on going back to being farmers. They kept their guns and their horses and took to robbing. They're mean sons-of-bitches; they'll kill lawmen as quick as a dog can lick a plate clean.'

'And no doubt they see themselves as plain, ordinary folk who do a little harmless stealing from the rich and defend themselves from the lawmen who work for those same rich,' Darrow drawled witheringly. 'Just like the James Gang.'

'How much did they get from the bank?' Pacey asked Turnage.

The lean undertaker poured hot coffee into tin mugs.

'The storekeeper, young Cooper, caught Dan Croucher's horse and brought it back with his bag of cash, so the bank got six hundred and fifty-five dollars back,' Josh said. He handed out the mugs of coffee. 'Harding wasn't exactly sure how much they got away with, but he reckons it's around two and a half thousand dollars. He'll give an exact figure tomorrow, when he's checked the books and counted up properly.'

'So Captain Tom Croucher gained two and a half thousand dollars, and lost his brother,' Pacey said. 'I wonder if he thinks it was worth it?'

'Would you call that a good deal?' Josh asked Darrow.

Darrow gave him an unfathomable look. 'That would depend on my hypothetical brother,' he said coolly.

No one thought he was joking.

2

The dull, grey February light did nothing to make the cell look more attractive. It wasn't even coming in through a window in the cell itself, but from a large, arched window on the other side of the long hall into which the tiered rows of cells faced. The heavy iron lattice work that formed the cell door cast a grid of pale shadows on the whitewashed walls. From the slanted angle of the shadows, and the emptiness in his stomach, Irish knew it was almost meal time.

The tall, heavy-set man stood and stretched, his grunt the only sound in the cell. His fair hair had been cut short by the prison authorities, though he still had a goatee. In spite of his size, his face was mild; he looked more like an ox than a bull. Irish turned and looked sadly at the occupant of the top bunk, who was curled up, facing the wall.

'Come on, Tomcat,' he said, his low voice gentle. 'Sure and it's nearly suppertime.'

Tomcat Billy didn't answer, didn't move.

'It ain't far, but it's out of here,' Irish coaxed. 'You can move and take a look right out the windows.'

Tomcat didn't respond. Irish fought down the urge to sigh.

In their first weeks here in Wyoming Territory Penitentiary, Tomcat had barely been able to keep still. He had paced about the cell, climbed up and down the bunks, and been the first one out and the last one in from the hour of exercise they had each day. Even the spells of labour around the prison hadn't helped. As the weeks had turned into months, Tomcat had gradually withdrawn into himself. Irish had watched helplessly as his quick, vivacious friend had turned into a silent shadow.

The door at the end of the hall

opened and guards entered.

'You've got to be after moving now,' Irish said firmly. Knowing that if Tomcat didn't move of his own accord, the guards would just drag him down, Irish reached up and simply lifted his friend from the top bunk and set him on his feet.

Tomcat Billy was slightly shorter than average and wiry: next to Irish, his head drooping, he looked small and frail. His green eyes had lost their usual sparkle, as though a light had been extinguished inside him. Tomcat had grown up in the wilds of Tennessee and had got his nickname from his agility in climbing and jumping. He loved to be outside: riding, climbing, swimming; free to move and be active. Spending more than twenty hours a day confined to the same small cell, with hardly even a glimpse of sky, had broken his roving spirit.

The guards were moving along the narrow wooden walkways outside the cells, unfastening the padlocks on the doors.

When their door was pulled open, Irish gave Tomcat a gentle push. The smaller man staggered slightly, then instinctively caught his balance in a graceful move. Tomcat kept going, his knee-high moccasins silent on the floor. Irish followed close behind as they filed along the walkway with the other prisoners, and down to the ground floor.

Here Tomcat finally raised his head to look at the high, arched windows. His pace slowed as he gazed at the open land and vast sky outside.

'Move along, you,' one of the guards ordered, coming closer. 'You ain't getting out there for another six years yet.'

Tomcat halted so abruptly Irish almost collided with him.

'Six years!' Tomcat exclaimed as though hearing the sentence for the first time. 'I can't. I won't! Not in here!' He glanced again at the window, then shook his head sharply. 'I can't!' he cried.

Struck with fear, Irish tried to grab him, but Tomcat moved too fast. He sprinted for the nearest open cell door and leapt for it. He caught the top with his hands and used the grille to climb swiftly upwards. From there he caught the arched bracket supporting the underside of the first walkway and swung himself up.

'Tomcat! Don't! No!' Irish yelled, looking up helplessly as his friend continued his frantic climb.

Guards and prisoners were shouting. Guards tried to force their way through the line of prisoners who were milling as they looked up, watching Tomcat's flight. Tomcat climbed the waist-high steel fence that edged the walkway. He balanced on the narrow rail that topped it and leapt for the walkway above. Irish's heart was hammering as he watched his friend pull himself up to the top floor. Tomcat grabbed an open cell door and climbed that. His short brown hair was almost brushing the ceiling, over thirty feet above the stone floor of the hall, and he could get no higher.

The open cell door filled almost the width of the walkway. Tomcat clung to the outer corner, hanging over the drop.

'No, Tomcat!' Irish yelled again, waving his arms. Guards were climbing the stairs at the side of the cell block, but it would take them precious time to reach Tomcat.

He didn't give them the time. Tomcat took one look down and jumped. He fell silently, tumbling towards the stone floor below. Other prisoners scattered but Irish stayed steady, his powerful arms outstretched to catch. Wiry though he was, Tomcat hit with enough force to knock Irish backwards. They landed on the ground together, Tomcat's fall cushioned by Irish's heavy body. Irish simply lay and gasped at first, half-winded by the impact. Other prisoners cheered and whooped as the guards tried to restore order.

At last, Irish recovered himself enough to raise his head. Tomcat lay huddled mostly atop him, sobbing. When Irish moved, Tomcat spoke softly.

'Why didn't you let me?'

'I couldn't let my friend be hurting himself,' Irish answered. 'And I'm not after being alone in here.'

Tomcat rolled off and curled up, hands clenched tight into fists. Irish sat up and glared at the guards who approached warily. Silently, he damned Sheriff Darrow and his deputies, who had captured them and so condemned Tomcat to this slow torture. It had taken just eight months inside for Tomcat to sink so low. Irish could see nothing in his future beyond watching his friend slowly disintegrate.

*   *   *

Darrow's black gelding slowed of its own accord, turning its head towards the house with the green fence out front. They were on Walnut Street, lined with substantial houses intended for the prosperous citizens the town was now producing. This house was one of the largest, with five steps leading up to a long veranda that ran the width of the wooden building. Large windows either side of the door were framed with velvet drapes, tied back to allow the sunlight of a fine March morning inside.

'All right, Gabriel,' Darrow said, with a rare smile as he turned his black horse towards the gate in the fence. 'For sure I shouldn't let you form bad habits, but I won't want to stop here when we get back. By then I reckon I'll be ready to go straight home.'

As Darrow dismounted, the front door opened and a young woman came out. She came slowly down the steps, holding the rail at the side. Even her full skirts and hoops, and the shawl draped loosely around herself, couldn't disguise the bulge of her advanced pregnancy. The sheriff raised his hat to her.

'Good morning, Minnie.' His rich voice was softer than when he spoke to his deputies.

Minnie Keating smiled back at him, pleasure lighting up her plain face. Her dress was stylish and expensive, and her dark blonde hair was carefully dressed, but she retained the unspoilt freshness that gave her charm.

'Good morning, sheriff,' she answered. 'Hugh said you were riding out around the county to check licences and collect taxes today.'

'That's correct. I believe there are two new saloons in Reddick, and others in Hampton City that need to renew their licences. It's not very exciting work,' Darrow added. 'But as Hugh would say, at least I'm not likely to get shot at.'

'It could happen,' Hugh said darkly, as he came out of the house to join them at the gate. 'Some hard-nosed chap decides he doesn't see why he should pay for the privilege of running a saloon selling terrible whiskey and weak beer, and you could have a gun in your belly.'

'At which point you'd hand over your

money to the saloonkeeper and toast him with his own atrocious whiskey,' Darrow remarked.

'Better that than getting shot in the belly,' Hugh promptly retorted.

The Englishman was almost as tall as the sheriff, but gave the impression of being smaller. His chestnut hair had receded a little at the front, and he had soft brown eyes that added to his general air of harmlessness. His usual clothing was good quality but unremarkable: brown trousers and boots, a soft-collared green shirt and a brown jacket. There was nothing much to distinguish him from other citizens of Govan until he spoke — his accent still upper-class English after several years out west.

Minnie neatly deflected any brewing argument.

'Did you bring any bread?' she asked her husband.

'Oh . . . er . . . yes.' He handed her a slice sprinkled with salt.

Darrow's black horse, Gabriel, snorted

gently and reached forward, his ears pricked. Minnie tore the slice in two and offered him one half on the palm of her hand. Gabriel took it delicately and chewed the bread with great pleasure.

'I declare, you're spoiling my horse, Miss Minnie,' Darrow said, patting his horse's neck. 'Every time we pass this house he wants to stop.'

Minnie looked at the sheriff then fed Gabriel the other piece of bread, a mischievous sparkle in her eyes. Darrow laughed.

'I'd better be going,' he said. He mounted, then raised his hat again in salute to Minnie. 'Hugh, I need the paperwork for that Yellow Valley rustling case ready for court tomorrow.'

'I'll get it done,' Hugh promised.

'Just be careful not to spill anything on it,' Darrow warned. 'I don't want to go to court with papers smelling of whiskey again. Judge Robinson damn nearly threw me out of the courtroom.'

'That was three years ago!' Hugh protested.

'It was three years too recent.'

Darrow turned his horse and rode away, with one last wave for Minnie.

She waved back, and as the sheriff departed, he heard her saying to her husband, 'I hope at least it was decent whiskey.'

As Darrow had expected, it was late afternoon and the sun was low before he got close to Govan again. The trail he was following joined another at a ford of the river a couple of miles north of town. Gabriel pricked his ears towards the water and snorted softly. Darrow patted his horse on the neck and turned it towards the river. They would be home before long, but there was no harm in letting his horse have a drink now. The sheriff slid from the saddle, wincing slightly as he landed. He moved stiffly for the few steps it took to lead Gabriel to the river bank; the long day in the saddle was taking its toll.

As the horse drank, Darrow looked about, gently stretching arms and legs in turn to ease his aches. Stands of trees and scrub lined the river banks, now showing the green flush of spring. Darrow thought about the court case on the following day, wondering if Hugh had got the paperwork organized properly. As he was thinking over the evidence in the case, something punched him hard in the chest.

Darrow crumpled on to the damp earth by the river, dimly aware that he'd just heard a rifle shot nearby. Gabriel snorted and moved a couple of paces away. Darrow lay on his back, looking up at the sky, his stunned mind gradually catching up. There was a sour, metallic taste in his mouth and he let his head roll to one side so blood could trickle out. The sheriff knew he'd been shot in the chest, but the shock was so great he barely felt pain, though he couldn't seem to move.

Splashing signalled danger in the back of his mind. After a moment he understood that the sound was of a horse wading out of the ford. It stopped close by and the rider dismounted, coming into Darrow's view. It was a man he'd seen before: a black-haired man with a long face cut across with strong brows. The man stood over Darrow, staring down at him bitterly. He kicked the sheriff in the side, watching his reaction. Darrow rocked slightly with the impact and moaned as pain shot through him. He let his eyes close and lay limply.

'I hear tell as Dan died as quick as blowing out a candle,' the man said. 'I sure hope you take some longer, killer-sheriff Darrow. I've been waiting here nigh on all day, waiting for you to come back to town. Didn't reckon as how you'd be so helpful, standing still to git yourself shot. Time anyone comes looking and finds you out here, you'll be long dead.' He paused, and sighed.

'I don't know if you can hear me, killer-sheriff, but you kilt my brother, Dan Croucher. I weren't at his burying and I likely won't ever see his grave. But I can put you in yours, Sheriff

30

Darrow, and now Dan kin rest easy in his.'

There was a soft rustle of clothing, then Darrow felt a tug at the front of his waistcoat. There was another slight pull, and a grunt of satisfaction. Darrow forced his eyes open and saw the man straightening up, a gold watch and chain dangling from his hand. For a moment, anger replaced the shock. Darrow's eyes blazed as he tried to push himself up. Tom Croucher simply planted one foot on Darrow's chest and pinned him down. The sheriff's strength abruptly faded, leaving him unable to struggle or even speak. He glared at the outlaw as Croucher swung the pocket watch on its chain. Darrow had never felt so helpless in his life as Croucher tucked the watch into his hip pocket. The burning pain in his chest, the humiliation of lying in the dirt at the outlaw's feet: all was forgotten in the bitterness of being unable to do anything as the watch — a precious link to his past — was taken from him.

Croucher bared his teeth in a humourless smile.

'Seems to me like you got more to worry about than me taking this purty watch.'

He shifted his foot slightly and pressed harder against the sheriff's chest. Agony burst through Darrow for a few moments until he mercifully passed out.

Tom Croucher spat, hitting the collar of Darrow's coat, mounted his horse and rode back across the river. Darrow never stirred.

3

Something brushed against Darrow's face. He opened his eyes back to a fuzzy consciousness and the coppery taste of blood in his mouth. A steady pain emanated from the right side of his chest. Gabriel was standing beside him, head lowered to look at him inquisitively. In a rush, Darrow remembered what had happened.

'Croucher,' he mumbled. It was a name he knew but it didn't mean anything to him at that moment.

Mentally steeling himself, Darrow rolled on to his left side. His jaw clenched tight as he fought against the pain and weakness. His nose and mouth were sticky and clogged with his blood. Darrow rested for a minute before trying to sit up. His vision greyed out for a few seconds, but eventually he was sitting, propping himself with shaky arms, every rasping breath painful.

When his head had cleared, and the pain had subsided to a level he could manage, Darrow considered his next moves. He couldn't have been unconscious for more than a few minutes. Darrow knew he'd lost a lot of blood already, and might not have regained consciousness if not for his horse's inquisitive nudges. His choices were clear: either wait here by the ford and hope someone came along in time to save him, or else to somehow get himself back to the town two miles away.

For Darrow, it was no choice. The only question was the matter of how he was going to make those two miles back to town.

'Gabriel.'

The black horse turned its head to the sound of his voice, and lowered it to peer at him. Darrow grabbed for one of the trailing reins and almost dropped it. He tightened his grip, dismayed by his own weakness but refusing to let the fear rise. He encouraged the horse to move forward, until it was standing closer to him.

'Sorry about this, Gabriel,' Darrow said. 'Steady now.'

Taking hold of the horse's foreleg, Darrow slowly pulled himself up until he had his feet underneath himself. Gabriel snorted and turned his head to see what his owner was doing, but stayed still. Darrow waited a moment until his head cleared, then reached for the stirrup. He clung to the stirrup and saddle as he stood, eventually leaning heavily against his patient horse. Darrow closed his eyes and permitted himself a moan of pain.

Eventually he felt some strength returning, but knew it might not last for long. He gathered the other rein and tied them both to the saddlehorn. Grasping the horn and cantle of the saddle, Darrow jumped and threw himself across his horse. Gabriel stepped back with surprise but the sheriff managed to cling on, belly-down across his saddle. When

Gabriel stood still, Darrow pulled and wriggled around until he was sitting properly. He slumped in the saddle for a minute, clinging to the horn as he waited for pain to subside and strength to return.

After a couple of minutes, Darrow stirred himself into action. His vision was greyish, his hands trembled and a part of him wanted nothing more than to give in and let unconsciousness take away the pain. A stronger part refused to relapse into the helplessness of before: fear of that vulnerability was stronger than the pain. Darrow spat fresh blood and slowly unfastened the length of rope he carried on his saddle. He tied one end around himself, looped it around the horn and under the flaps of the saddle-bags behind him, then back on his other side to the horn again.

Letting out a long, painful breath, Darrow picked up the reins and closed his legs against his horse's sides.

'Come on, Gabriel.' The words were slurred. 'Home.'

The black horse took an uncertain step and halted, confused by its rider's weak aids. Darrow stirred himself to press harder and Gabriel began to walk. The horse turned towards Govan without being asked and walked steadily on. Darrow took a good hold of his mane and gritted his teeth, steeling himself to fight off the weakness for as long as possible.

★ ★ ★

Minnie rolled the ivory dice.

'Four and a two,' she said thoughtfully, studying the backgammon board.

Hugh rapidly calculated her options and waited anxiously to see what she would do. Minnie picked up a black counter, moving it two places, then moved yet another four places round the board and picked it up with a triumphant smile.

'That's four I've borne off and you haven't made one yet,' she pointed out to her husband.

Hugh gave her a mock scowl, annoyed at the fact that she was ahead, but pleased that his wife liked to play and was good enough to challenge him.

'I'm using a subtle strategy,' he claimed. 'You wait till we get to the end game.'

'That shouldn't take long, at the rate I'm beating you,' Minnie answered. 'Now roll your dice and get on with it.'

As Hugh picked up his own pair of dice, they heard a horse whinnying outside. Minnie took no notice, but Hugh paused, the dice in his hand.

'Go on, roll them,' Minnie urged.

'That sounded like Gabriel,' Hugh said, looking towards the window though the curtains were now drawn.

Minnie glanced at the French clock ticking on the mantelpiece. 'I'd reckon the sheriff would go straight to the livery barn if he wasn't back until now. He must be tired.'

The horse whinnied again and Hugh stood up.

'It does sound like Gabriel, and it

sounds like he's right outside.'

He moved to the bay window and peered behind the curtain into the dark street.

'There's a dark horse at the gate, but I don't think it has a rider,' he said, trying to remember if he'd left his gunbelt on the coat stand in the hall. 'No, there is something in the saddle.'

The horse tossed its head with a distinctive circling motion that Gabriel used. Hugh's stomach tightened with sudden fear. He took a deep breath, trying to calm himself, and disentangled himself from the curtain. Hugh mustered a smile for Minnie, who was watching him.

'What is it?' she asked, not fooled by the smile.

'I think that is Gabriel, and something's wrong,' Hugh answered, crossing the room to the door.

Minnie rose too but Hugh put out his hand to stop her following.

'I don't know what's wrong,' he said. 'I want you to stay in here and away from the windows.'

Minnie frowned slightly but sat down again, looking at her husband.

'Call Baird to go with you,' she suggested.

Baird was the groom/gardener and lived in a couple of rooms above the stables out back of the house.

'I'll call you when I know what's happening,' he promised.

'Take care,' Minnie said.

Moving into the hall, Hugh was pleased to find his gunbelt hanging beneath his jacket. He strapped it on, and checked the loads in the powerful Webley revolver he preferred. With the gun in one hand, he quickly pulled open the door, moving with it so it covered him.

'Who's there?' he called, trying to sound bold.

When no shots were fired, he peered further round the door. Soft light from the lamp hanging in the hall spilled out down the steps to the gate. The horse there snorted, a familiar sound.

'Darrow? Is that you?' Hugh called. His skin prickled, but he had no idea what was wrong. He was very tempted to slam the door and lock it, hoping the mystery would go away. Instead, he stepped back and asked Minnie to bring him a lamp from the parlour.

Gun in one hand, lamp in the other, he made his way cautiously down the short path to the gate. Hugh spoke gently to the horse, trying to mask his jumping nerves. It wasn't completely dark yet, and as Hugh's eyes adjusted, he saw the figure slumped along the horse's neck. He holstered his gun and held the lantern up near the sheriff's face. The yellow light revealed a horrifying mask of dark, congealed blood around Darrow's nose and mouth. Hugh recoiled, the lantern swinging in his hand and sending long shadows dancing across the horse and its motionless rider.

'Hugh! What is it?' Minnie called from the doorway.

Hugh swallowed, taking deep breaths

to try and calm himself.

'Darrow,' he said weakly. 'He's . . . someone's . . . '

He glanced back at Minnie and the sight of her gave him the courage to act. Stepping close and lifting the lantern again, he put his free hand against Darrow's face. To his relief, he felt the faintest stirring of breath across the back of his hand. Hugh's hopes suddenly rose and he turned to his wife.

'Send Baird out here to help me and ask Teresa to fetch Doc Travis — urgently!'

★   ★   ★

'What's happened? How's the sheriff?' Deputy Pacey was asking questions as he entered the Keatings' parlour, some half an hour later.

'Doc Travis is upstairs with him now,' Hugh answered. 'He's removing the bullet.' He shuddered slightly and took a slug from the tumbler of whiskey he was holding. 'Drink?' he asked Pacey, who was sitting down.

Pacey gave Hugh's glass a cool look. 'Coffee, please.'

Minnie started to struggle up from her armchair, but Hugh waved her back and strode to the door. Leaning through, he called to the English lady's maid who had shown Pacey into the parlour.

'Nettie, bring coffee, please. Two cups,' he added, after a glance at his tumbler. Another swift gulp emptied it as he came back into the room. Setting the glass down on the sideboard, Hugh took the armchair next to Minnie's.

'So what exactly happened to Darrow?' Pacey asked, leaning forward. 'Your message didn't explain anything.'

'Gabriel brought him back here.' Hugh went on to explain how they'd found the unconscious sheriff tied to his saddle and tended to him. Doc Travis had found the single gunshot wound in Darrow's chest, and was treating it now with the help of Teresa, the cook-general.

'Just the one wound?' Pacey asked.

Hugh nodded. 'I checked Darrow's guns and neither have been fired today. I don't think he had any bruises but there was so much blood it was hard to see.' He cast a quick glance at the whiskey glass, just out of reach. Minnie put her hand on his arm and he gave her a weak smile of gratitude.

'So it was an ambush,' Pacey concluded. 'They must have been after the tax money.'

'Yes. No!' Hugh stood and hurried to the other end of the room. He reached down beside a bookcase and returned with a pair of saddle-bags slung over his shoulder. 'Blaine brought these in after he stabled Gabriel,' he explained. 'They're heavy,' he added, heaving them on to the table, beside the abandoned backgammon game.

Pacey and Minnie joined him as he unbuckled the saddle-bags. Inside was a notebook and a dozen neatly labelled, mostly full, cloth moneybags.

'This looks fairly complete,' Pacey mused. The tall deputy picked out one of the moneybags, bouncing it gently on the palm of his hand. It chinked softly.

Hugh was looking at the notebook. 'There's a record of everything Darrow collected today.' He paused for a moment, thinking, then shoved the notebook into Pacey's hands. 'Check the bags against the notes; see if everything's there. I'll be back in a minute.' He hurried out of the room and upstairs.

A couple of minutes later he was back, holding a black leather pocketbook.

'There's still money in this,' Hugh said. 'The only thing missing is Darrow's watch.'

'Why would anyone shoot a man just for his watch, and leave everything else?' Minnie asked. 'They might not have known he was carrying the taxes, but surely they'd have taken cash money, and Gabriel's a good horse.'

'If they didn't shoot Darrow just to steal from him, it must have been someone with a grudge against him,' Pacey suggested.

'That doesn't narrow down the list of suspects,' Hugh remarked, before recollecting the situation and casting a guilty glance up in the direction of the bedroom where Darrow was.

Pacey closed the notebook and put it back in the saddle-bag. 'We know where Darrow went today and what his likely route was. We need to get out there now and look for evidence.'

Hugh glanced at the closed curtains. 'It's dark.'

'So we'll take lanterns. You take these saddle-bags to the office and lock them in the safe: I'll find Whiskers and bring him along to read sign. And we should get someone to be in the office while we're out, maybe Turnage. I'll meet you at the livery stables.' Pacey, brisk and decisive, put his hand on Hugh's shoulder and pushed him towards the door.

Hugh baulked, a stubborn look coming into his eyes. 'You're not in charge here.'

Pacey hesitated in his stride, taken by

surprise. Hugh followed up his brief advantage.

'I'm the senior deputy,' Hugh insisted. 'If the sheriff's not available, I'm in charge. And I say it's plain stupid to go out there in the dark. For one thing, we'd probably trample more tracks than we'd find. Besides, what if the shooter came back? If we go out in the dark, waving lanterns around, we might as well pin targets on our chests.'

Pacey's expression admitted that Hugh had a point, but his posture was unyielding.

'If you're in charge, then you'd better decide what we're going to do.' He folded his arms and waited for Hugh's response with a look of studied patience.

Hugh took a deep breath, his mind spinning. He knew Pacey was waiting for him to make a fool of himself, and only the desire to confound the younger man stopped him from babbling out the first things that came to his mind. As he thought, he caught Minnie's eye. Her confident smile calmed him and a moment later, Nettie appeared with the coffee. As they all sat down, and took their cups, Hugh began to make plans.

'You can take the saddle-bags back to the office,' he told Pacey. 'Call on Whiskers and let him know you'll both be heading out at first light to look for evidence.'

'You're going to stay safe here in town?' Pacey asked.

'Someone needs to stay in town,' Hugh pointed out. 'And besides, Darrow was due to go to court tomorrow about that rustling case. I'll have to do it now.'

'We'll need to find another deputy,' Pacey said. 'Three's barely enough to manage as it is, and with Darrow, well . . . '

'I'll wire Laramie,' Hugh said shortly, and sipped his coffee.

They talked a few minutes more as the coffee was drunk. The conversation got increasingly sporadic and ceased altogether as heavy footsteps were heard coming down the stairs. All three were staring expectantly at the door as Doc Travis entered the parlour. His face and hands were freshly washed and clean, but there was a dark smudge of blood on his shirt collar.

'He's alive,' the doctor announced bluntly.

Minnie gave a sigh of relief but Hugh still felt sick in his stomach.

'How . . . ?' He stumbled over the words.

'I can't guarantee anything,' Travis said. 'He's lost a helluva lot of blood. If he makes it through the night, he's got a fair chance of pulling through, but that's only if he don't develop an infection. I know you like to gamble, Hugh, but if I'm honest, I don't reckon I'd lay odds on Darrow making it.'

'He will,' Hugh said boldly. 'Someone shot Darrow because they wanted to kill him, but you know what he's like. He never does anything just because someone else wants him to, and that includes dying.'

4

The next few days proved Hugh to be right. In spite of his injury, Darrow refused to die and two days later was sitting up in bed, telling Hugh what had happened. Hugh sent Pacey out to look for Croucher and wired the US Marshal's office about the attack. The shooting was reported in newspapers throughout Wyoming and Colorado. For all his stubborn spirit, Darrow's survival was largely down to careful nursing. Three weeks passed before Doc Travis agreed that he could return to the quarters above the law office that he shared with Pacey and even then the doctor might not have agreed if Minnie hadn't been so close to the expected arrival of her baby.

Darrow needed a day's bed rest after the move across town, but the day after, he insisted on getting up. He interviewed the temporary deputy, Seth Baldwin, and gave grudging approval. Every day he went out for a walk; just a few minutes at first but increasing the distance each day. If the sheriff was moved by the good wishes of the town folk he met, he demonstrated no more than polite thanks. His expression was sterner than usual and he carried a brooding presence, like a gathering thunderstorm. Hugh made sure to carry out his duties with unusual efficiency.

★　★　★

Hugh paused just inside the livery barn, letting his eyes adjust to the lower light level. Norman, the barn owner, looked out from the saddle room, a bridle dangling from one hand and a rag in the other.

'Hello,' Hugh greeted him. 'I'm looking for Darrow.'

'He's here,' the black man replied. 'Been talking to his horse a little while now.'

'Oh, thanks,' Hugh replied. He raised a hand in thanks and headed deeper into the livery barn, between the rows of box stalls.

Darrow was inside Gabriel's box, leaning against the wooden partition in an uncharacteristically casual pose. Hugh knew Darrow well enough to recognize the slight signs of strain in his face, and knew that the casual stance was a reluctant concession to the sheriff's physical weakness. Darrow snapped a carrot in two and offered one piece to his horse. Gabriel took the treat and crunched it, turning an ear in Hugh's direction. Darrow followed his horse's cue, and saw Hugh outside the stall.

'You don't usually come here just to visit,' Hugh remarked.

'Neither do you,' Darrow answered sharply. 'Do you have a reason to come and plague me here?'

Darrow's glare was interrupted by Gabriel gently nuzzling him. 'I owe you my life,' Darrow said to Gabriel, giving him the rest of the carrot. He patted the horse on the neck. 'Your bad habit of stopping at Hugh's house was lucky for me.'

Hugh watched him for a moment before speaking. 'I came looking for you because I thought you'd like to know how the rustling trial's going.'

Justice Robinson had adjourned the trial for a few days after the attack on Darrow. Hugh found the detail of court cases dull, and was usually happy to leave that side of things to Darrow, who had studied law before the Civil War.

'You remembered the instructions I gave you?' Darrow inquired.

'I think I made a pretty good job of it,' Hugh said, looking pleased with himself. 'I presented the evidence well and I think Justice Robinson was impressed.'

'Surprised, more likely, if you were that good,' Darrow interrupted.

Hugh pretended he hadn't heard. 'Robinson hasn't given the verdict yet, but from the way he looked, I bet he's going to find them guilty. Though Walker may have made it worse for them when he spat at Robinson and called him a sawn-off, louse-infested son of a three-legged dancing skunk.'

A rare smile flashed briefly across Darrow's face. 'I sure admire to have seen that,' he admitted. He fell silent again, absently stroking his horse's neck. When he spoke, the suddenness startled Hugh. 'Has there been any word about Croucher?'

Hugh suddenly looked guilty. 'Oh, er, yes.' He winced at Darrow's glare, and continued. 'Whiskers sent over a telegram when I was in the office. It was from Sheriff, er, the sheriff of Dereham County, in Colorado. Croucher robbed a stagecoach down there. Sheriff . . . um . . . lost track of him over towards Boulder.'

Again, there was silence before Darrow spoke.

'Pacey tells me that Baldwin has the makings of a good lawman.'

Hugh nodded. 'He seems a decent chap.'

'Make his post permanent then.'

Hugh raised his eyebrows. 'Four lawmen in town? I know we need more but Robinson's sure to object unless it's discussed by the council first.'

'Deputy sheriff is a county post: the town council has no say in who I appoint,' Darrow answered. He looked directly at Hugh. 'In any case, there won't be four lawmen in Govan. I'll be in Colorado.'

'Colorado?' Hugh blinked. 'Oh, chasing Croucher? Well, we can't go after him until you're a lot stronger. You know what Doc Travis said when he saw you last . . . '

'We aren't going after Croucher,' Darrow interrupted. 'I am going after Croucher alone.'

Hugh straightened up. 'You can't do that; it's too dangerous. I mean what if you have an accident: how are you going to get help? And Croucher has men riding with him. You'll be outnumbered. You'll need help, at least one other, preferably two or three.'

Darrow's dark eyes bored into him. 'I don't need help. I don't need anyone and I definitely don't need you.'

There was hurt in Hugh's expressive eyes, but he didn't reply immediately. He studied Darrow before speaking. 'You believe that if you want.'

Darrow turned away. His saturnine face betrayed no feelings but his hand gently caressed the patient black horse.

'When were you going to tell me that you plan to resign as sheriff?'

Darrow straightened and turned, his movement so abrupt that his horse threw its head up in momentary alarm. He recovered in moments, glaring at his deputy.

Hugh's teeth showed in a humourless smile. 'Oh, don't worry; no one else in town can ever predict what you're likely to do. You're still a mystery to them.'

'But not, apparently, to you,' Darrow drawled. 'How humiliating to realize that my intentions can be read by a dissipated gambler whose own family thought it was worth spending the money to exile him on another continent.'

'You've met my brother; what makes you think I was sorry to leave?' Hugh retorted.

Darrow relaxed. 'So go ahead; dazzle me with the brilliance of your deductions.'

'Well, you've got no legal jurisdiction in Colorado, so you can't go there officially. It's a big state and there's no guarantee he'll even stay in Colorado. It could take you weeks or months to find him, if you ever do. You can't take that time and be sheriff of Govan county, because you won't *be* in Govan county, therefore you'll have to resign the post. Besides, you like things to be tidy and organized, so you wouldn't just go off and leave us without a sheriff and not knowing whether to expect you back anytime. You're not even sure if you'll make it back,' Hugh added more slowly. 'You don't want me along because you think you'll be chasing Croucher for months, and because you think one or both of us will get killed, and I'm married now.'

Darrow ducked his head slightly: it was enough to tell Hugh that he was right.

'Why is catching Croucher so important that it's worth leaving Govan for?' Hugh asked.

'That's my business.' Darrow's hand involuntarily moved to the waistcoat pocket he had kept his watch in.

Hugh didn't miss the significance of the gesture. 'Why is a watch worth possibly getting yourself killed?'

Darrow's dark eyes smouldered with emotion but he answered the question, almost as if he couldn't help himself. 'It was a gift from . . . a friend, just before I joined my regiment.'

'It was from a woman, wasn't it?'

Darrow didn't speak, but the answer was in his face.

Hugh waited, hoping he would talk, but Darrow remained silent and Hugh knew better than to keep pushing him.

'Croucher's a thief,' Hugh said. 'He

steals things in order to sell them. You should contact jewellery shops and pawn shops. He probably sold your watch as soon as he needed some cash.'

Darrow shook his head. 'He could have taken money, or Gabriel, if he wanted valuables. Croucher didn't shoot me in order to steal from me.' His face darkened. 'He hunted me, then took a trophy to mark his kill. And I, I was foolish enough to react and let him know it was important to me.'

'You'd just been shot; you can't blame yourself for not thinking straight right at that moment.'

'I made mistakes.' Darrow's voice was harsh. 'I let him ambush me and I let him know I valued that watch.'

Hugh bravely ignored the warning signs of Darrow's temper. 'Going after Croucher alone would be another mistake,' he declared, then held his breath.

Somewhat to his surprise, Darrow didn't immediately contradict or dismiss him. Instead, the sheriff carefully leaned back against the lumber partition of the box stall, looking weary. His dark eyes were thoughtful as he studied his friend.

'Why would it be a mistake?' he drawled, with deceptive mildness.

Hugh breathed out in a long, quiet sigh.

'I've been reading all the old notices and newspaper pieces I can find on Captain Croucher. Have you ever been to Colorado?'

'No.' Darrow gave Hugh a look of long-suffering patience.

Hugh continued, undaunted. 'Most of Croucher's robberies have been in Colorado, but he's also been identified at robberies in Utah, New Mexico and Kansas. That's one hell of a large area. He's never really got close to being caught because he keeps moving on. He knows mountain passes, hidden canyons, places where he can shelter or get supplies. Croucher's been running rings around the law for over ten years.

'You don't know those territories and

you won't have time to learn them like Croucher has. When you got shot, your picture was in newspapers from Wyoming to Utah. As soon as you go to Colorado, you'll be recognized and Croucher will hear that you're after him. If he decides to run, you'll be chasing a will o' the wisp all over the west. More likely, he'll decide to finish the job and hunt *you* down.'

Darrow didn't immediately reply; he folded his arms and stared across the box stall at his horse, brooding.

'You can't go after him,' Hugh repeated. 'You're far more likely to die than he is, so why give him the satisfaction?'

Darrow turned his dark eyes on his deputy. 'I can't just let him go.'

Hugh thought for a moment. 'You can't go yourself, so you'll have to send or hire someone else.' His expression brightened. 'Hire a man-hunter who knows the territory. Let them do all the hard work and take the risks.'

'That's your preferred philosophy of

life, isn't it?' Darrow's words were quiet and lacked their usual sting.

Hugh looked at him thoughtfully. 'You definitely won't be going after him unless you get home and rest now. If you faint, I'm not dragging you back along Main Street.'

'I'm glad to know that my dignity would be spared by your laziness.' Darrow slowly straightened, patted his horse in farewell, and left the box.

'I want to get Croucher myself,' Darrow said as they walked. 'For sure I may need a bounty hunter to catch him but I'll deal with Croucher personally. Though if a lawman can't get to Croucher, I don't reckon a known bounty hunter's got a much better chance. There's got to be some way to get to him; a new tactic.'

'Well, if the law's no use, that leaves criminals,' Hugh remarked. 'Set a thief to catch a thief, or something.'

Darrow raised an eyebrow. 'Do you happen to know any trustworthy thieves I can send after a vicious killer?'

Hugh shrugged. 'Not right now.'

Darrow and Hugh left the livery barn at a leisurely pace, emerging into the spring sunshine. The breeze brought the smell of soap and steam from the back of the bath house as they passed it. As they reached the crossroads, Hugh pointed over to the funeral parlour.

'I saw Josh the other evening, while I was out doing the rounds.'

'Rehearsing some new overwrought melodrama with the Amateur Players?'

Hugh shook his head. 'He was escorting a woman to the Full Plate Restaurant. He had his arm through hers!'

A smile softened Darrow's features. 'Well now, do you think she knows he's a mortician?'

'It's not the sort of thing you can hide for very long,' Hugh pointed out. 'Especially when your name's in fancy letters on the shop window.'

'Do you know who his young lady was?'

Hugh shook his head. 'It was pretty dark by then and I didn't want to get close and stare. Being an undertaker makes things tough enough without . . . '

He was interrupted by someone shouting his name. Baird was on the other side of the street, waving his arms. As Hugh saw him, he ran into the street, dodging a pair of mules pulling a farm wagon. Hugh moved towards him, his heart suddenly beating faster. Baird made it safely across the street and halted, breathing heavily.

'Minnie's ma sent me to fetch you,' he gasped.

Hugh's face paled. 'It's started? The baby?'

Baird nodded. 'Mrs Davis said to tell you everything's fine; she don't want the doctor getting in the way right now. Ain't nothing much gonna happen for a few hours yet.'

Hugh blinked, and looked at Darrow, who had joined them. 'I should be with Minnie; at home, anyway. I want to be right there in case, well . . . '

Darrow smiled and clapped him on the shoulder. 'You go on home, and give Minnie my good wishes. Why, I'm sure it'll be all right.'

'Thanks.' Hugh jumped down off the boardwalk and hurried away, the problem of Croucher instantly forgotten.

5

'Last night was a farce,' Darrow snapped. 'You arrested eight drunks . . . '

'I had to!' Pacey interrupted. 'They were all disturbing the peace and one pair were shooting at store signs. Or trying to. It's a goddam miracle they didn't shoot anyone out on the street.'

'So you put eight men in cells meant to hold four, one of them vomited over two others and they got to fighting.' Darrow sighed. 'It's a perfect example of why we need to expand the law facilities in this town, if only the council will agree.'

Further comment was interrupted as the office door opened.

Hugh entered, carrying a covered basket in one hand, with Josh Turnage behind him. Darrow rose and went to greet him, Pacey following. Hugh was smiling, his eyes bright, as he shook hands with the other lawmen and received their congratulations. He'd sent a note first thing in the morning, announcing the successful delivery of a baby girl late the previous night. The baby had taken over a whole day to arrive, so the news had been greeted with relief.

'Yes, Minnie's doing well,' he said, answering a question from the sheriff. 'She's tired, but Doc Travis saw her last night and said she's fine. Her mother says so too.'

'Well now, Mrs Davis has had four children herself, so I guess she knows what she's talking about,' Darrow said.

Hugh suddenly remembered the basket he was carrying and set it on the desk. Removing the green-and-white gingham cover, he took out a bottle of champagne, glasses and a sponge cake.

'There'll be a formal christening later, of course,' Hugh said, looking around at the others. 'But I wanted to . . . well, share something with my friends now.'

Turnage cut slices of the deep, jam-filled cake, while Hugh carefully opened the champagne and filled the glasses. Each man took a glass, and Hugh raised his high. He straightened, reaching his true height for once, and spoke clearly.

'Gentlemen. To my wife, Minnie, and our first child, Rose Victoria Keating.'

'To Minnie and Rose.'

The formal toast was drunk, then the glasses were topped up and the cake sampled. Hugh modestly accepted congratulations and promised to pass on messages of good will to Minnie. The conversation flowed into a lively discussion on the merits of different alcoholic drinks. A few minutes on, the talk was interrupted by the appearance of Homer, the law office cat. The handsome young ginger cat had been rescued by Hugh, but stubbornly took to Darrow. He liked to curl up on the sheriff's lap in the evenings while Darrow pretended to be indifferent to it.

Homer jumped easily on to the leather-topped desk and stretched his nose towards the cake.

'That's too good for you,' Josh said,

picking the cat up and putting it on the floor in one smooth motion. 'You stick to mice.'

'That reminds me,' Hugh said, pointing at Darrow. 'Tomcat Billy and Irish.'

Darrow looked at him. 'Two of the gang that stole your family's jewellery before your wedding.'

Hugh nodded. 'The trustworthy thieves you wanted. I was thinking about it yesterday, trying to distract myself, you know.'

'Trustworthy thieves?' said Pacey.

'Set a thief to catch a thief,' Hugh answered. 'Darrow can't go after Croucher himself, so I said he needed a thief to do the chasing. Croucher would trust another outlaw — more than he'd trust other folk anyway.'

'And then what happens?' Pacey asked scornfully.

Hugh began to look flustered. 'Well, our thief finds out where Croucher is and wires Darrow, so he can quickly find Croucher and arrest him.'

'That almost makes sense,' Josh said.

Pacey laughed. 'What makes you think that some two-bit thief is going to help out the law? They'll just run and you'll never see them again. More dangerous people who should be locked up will be on the loose.'

'Tomcat Billy and Irish aren't dangerous,' Hugh insisted. He looked at Darrow and Josh. 'You remember them? They weren't the dangerous ones in that gang; they weren't wanted for killing anyone. They weren't that sort.'

'Maybe not,' Darrow answered. 'But I surely wouldn't trust either of them if we set them loose and you'd be a fool if you did.'

For once, Hugh stuck to his guns. 'I think they're worth trusting. They co-operated before, remember? They told us where the tiaras were buried in return for having the attempted murder charges dropped. Tomcat hated the idea of spending years inside the jail. He'd do almost anything to be let out.'

'So when you let him out, he vanishes,' Pacey said, walking towards

Hugh and circling round him. 'You are a fool.'

Hugh twisted to keep Pacey in sight, then dismissed him and turned back to Darrow. 'Those two are friends, aren't they? Irish fretted over Tomcat when he got hurt when he was arrested. He surrendered at once instead of trying to escape on his own. You could release one, and keep the other in prison as surety for his return.'

Pacey started to speak again but Darrow held up a hand for silence. Darrow studied Hugh thoughtfully, then smiled.

'You're sure set on this, aren't you?' he drawled.

Hugh looked faintly suspicious. 'You want Croucher brought in, but we know you can't go after him yourself. So you have to get someone to do it for you.'

'There are manhunters for hire,' Josh remarked.

'They cost money,' Hugh said promptly. 'Tomcat Billy and Irish would do it for expenses.'

It was a shrewd comment. Darrow

spoke very little of his past, simply saying that his family had lost everything in the Civil War and its aftermath. As Govan had grown more prosperous, so had its sheriff, though only Hugh had any idea how much extra Darrow had acquired through unrecorded fines and other low-key illegalities.

The sheriff frowned, looking uncharacteristically uncertain.

Pacey spun to face him. 'You're surely not thinking of going along with this foolishness! Since when did Hugh have any good ideas?'

Darrow stared coolly at him. 'Now and again, he does make sense.'

Hugh stood a little straighter and looked smugly at Pacey.

Josh spoke up. 'I'd trust Tomcat Billy and Irish.'

Pacey scowled at him too, but Darrow spoke first. He pointed at his tall deputy.

'Pacey, go out and find Baldwin. Tell him to come back here for his share of Hugh's gifts, and take over his patrol until he's done here.'

Pacey glared at him, his eyes blazing. Darrow stared back, profoundly unimpressed.

After staring in silent defiance a few moments longer, Pacey stalked swiftly across the office to pick up his hat and a shotgun and left, closing the door sharply behind himself. Hugh let out a quiet sigh of relief. Darrow moved behind the desk and sat down. Hugh promptly took the nearest chair and Josh took the other.

'I don't have the authority to make a deal to release Tomcat and Irish,' Darrow drawled. 'I'd need the co-operation of the prison governor and maybe the judge that sentenced them.'

'Can't hurt to ask,' Hugh said. 'You'll just have to remember to ask nicely, instead of demanding, as you usually do,' he added.

Darrow chose to ignore the latter comment. 'They may say I can't use convicted criminals for a personal matter.'

'It's not just about your personal

vengeance though,' Josh said. 'Croucher is a notorious criminal. He's stolen tens of thousands of dollars since the war and killed, what, a dozen people? No lawman's caught him yet.'

'Besides, the authorities don't want Croucher or any other outlaw getting the idea they can go around shooting lawmen in the back,' Hugh put in. 'I certainly don't like the idea,' he added with characteristic self-interest.

Darrow smiled suddenly. 'I surely can't imagine you do.' He leaned back in his chair, thinking. 'I reckon Tomcat and Irish will work better as a team. Like you said, they're friends. If Croucher even suspects they're working for the law, they'll be as dead as beef. Together, they've got a better chance of pulling it off.'

'All round, it's one hell of a gamble,' Josh said. 'Do you trust them enough?'

'I don't trust many people, but I don't reckon I've got much choice.'

Irish followed the prison guard along the corridor. Tomcat shambled along beside him, occasionally bumping into him and staggering slightly. The guards no longer bothered cursing Tomcat or ordering him to walk properly. Most of the time he never seemed to hear what anyone said to him, and he suffered blows with silent indifference, as though he didn't understand what was happening. Irish steadied him when necessary and kept walking quietly, wondering why they'd been summoned.

When they were led into the warden's office, the first thing Irish noticed was the opulence of it, so different to the rest of the prison. Most of the floor was covered by a carpet, intricately patterned in reds and blue. The furniture was good quality, including a walnut-veneered desk with fat, leather-bound books on the top. Even the walls were papered, like a room in a fancy hotel. Then Irish looked at and recognized the two men sitting on the other side of a small table and he stiffened.

The sheriff, Darrow, stared back with characteristic intensity and self-assurance. His deputy, Keating, had a softer, rounder face. There was a slight wariness in the way he looked at the two prisoners, as though he expected an attack. At the sight of them, Irish's big hands automatically clenched into fists, a move that didn't escape Darrow's notice. Then Irish saw the way the deputy was staring at Tomcat. The deputy looked puzzled, then concerned and there was guilt in his soft, brown eyes.

During the long, grey months, as Tomcat had got sicker, Irish had concentrated his despair down into a burning resentment towards the men who had captured them. He'd built up a vision of them as heartless, uncaring about the fate of the men they'd sent to jail. The shock on Keating's face as he looked at Tomcat didn't fit with the idea of him that Irish had built up. Confused, Irish let his broad shoulders slump.

At a brisk gesture from Darrow, the

guards left the room, leaving the four men alone. Darrow glanced at Tomcat, his sharp eyes assessing and momentarily compassionate, before he looked back at Irish, as focussed as ever.

'Have you heard of Captain Tom Croucher?' Darrow asked.

The unexpected question made Irish pause and think for a moment.

'Sure an' I've heard of him,' he answered warily. 'I've never met him to speak to.'

Darrow looked at Tomcat, who was gazing blankly at the wall. 'What about him?'

'The same,' Irish answered simply.

'What do you mean by 'not met him to speak to'?' Keating asked.

'We've been in the same town at the same time a couple o' times,' Irish explained. 'I've been after seeing Croucher and his brother in a saloon, playing faro. Didn't have no reason to go speak to him.'

'You weren't interested in riding with him?' Darrow asked.

Irish shook his head. 'He's a killer

and we're not,' he answered firmly. 'Sure and I know that stealing's a sin, but it ain't the same as killing someone and the Crouchers are too damn quick to shoot.'

The two lawmen glanced at one another. Keating half-smiled, looking pleased with himself: Darrow looked thoughtful. The sheriff looked at Tomcat.

'Is he ill?'

The question briefly revived the anger Irish had felt towards the lawmen. Even as his powerful muscles tensed, he was trying to figure out the best way to answer. He had no idea why these lawmen were talking to him about Tom Croucher or what they wanted, but they wanted something from him and Tomcat. Irish only wanted to protect and help his friend. The lawmen might find some way of helping Tomcat if they knew he was ill, or they might think he was no use to them, and would just send him back to his cell. As Irish hesitated, he met the sheriff's sharp gaze, and knew there was no point in outright lying.

'He's not after being well,' Irish admitted. 'It's being locked up.' He turned and looked at his friend, feeling the usual pain at seeing Tomcat so listless. 'He's needing to get out and see the sky when he wants, to have space about himself. It's like keeping a wild mustang in a box stall for months. Being caged in prison's just about broke his spirit,' Irish finished sadly.

'Would he be all right if he were released?' Keating asked.

Irish's heart seemed to stop for a moment. 'Why, yes. Yes I'm plumb sure o' that!'

Darrow gave Keating a hard look before addressing Irish again.

'Croucher is believed to be in Colorado at the present,' the sheriff said. 'Do you think you could find him?'

Irish nodded. 'Now that I surely could.' He was working hard to keep his face as placid as usual, but there was a tight knot of excitement building inside his stomach.

'Last fall, Croucher and his gang

raided the bank in Govan,' Darrow said.

He explained about the raid, Dan Croucher's death, and about the ambush that had so nearly killed him.

'I can't leave Govan long enough to go chasing after Tom Croucher,' Darrow concluded, his dark eyes fixing Irish's gaze. 'If you two make contact with Croucher and pass back information that leads to his arrest or death, you'll both be pardoned for the robbery and released permanently. If you break oath and run, every lawman west of the Mississippi will be on the lookout for you, you will be caught, and you'll spend the rest of your miserable lives locked up, understand?'

'I'll do it!' Tomcat Billy said. The others stared, startled to hear him speak. His voice was raspy, as though unused for a long time, but his green eyes were burning brightly in his pinched face. 'I'll do whatever the hell you want. Just let me out!'

6

Tomcat dug his heels into his horse's sides and whooped as it leapt forward into a gallop. Irish yelled and urged his horse after him. They raced south across the high prairie, with the Rocky Mountains rising skywards to the west and the great sweep of open prairie to the east. The short buffalo grass was springy underfoot and wildflowers danced cheerfully in the endless wind that blew across the prairie. As they topped a rise, they saw a herd of pronghorns in the near distance. Within seconds, the whole herd was on the move, the deer bounding away gracefully at a pace far faster than the horses could match. Tomcat yelled and let his horse race down the slope, slowing it to a walk when it reached the bottom. Irish caught up a moment later, as Tomcat patted his blowing horse on the neck.

Tomcat looked a little fragile, to his friend, but his green eyes were glowing with a brilliance that had been missing for months. Hearing him laugh was a relief that brought a smile to Irish's broad face.

'I can't hardly believe I'm really out here,' Tomcat said, his gaze turning to the wide horizons. 'I keep thinking it must be a dream and I'm gonna wake up back in that cell.' His eyes clouded momentarily at the memories.

'For sure it's awake you are now,' Irish reassured him. 'I can be giving you a pinch if you like.'

Tomcat laughed and reined his horse a couple of steps away. 'No thanks!'

He nudged the dun mare on, Irish following suit. Tomcat looked sideways at him.

'I should have said this 'fore now, but thanks for being a friend in there. I'd surely never have made it without you looking out for me; I'm beholden to you.'

'Well now, you'd have done the same

for me,' Irish replied simply.

It was the deputy, Keating, who had pointed out that they would need to have a plausible excuse for being released from prison so early. While neither Tomcat Billy nor Irish were well-known criminals, they were known among other outlaws, and news of their arrest and sentencing would have been passed around. There was no good reason for them to be pardoned, and the case against them had been clear enough that there was no obvious technicality that could be exploited. After some consultation with the prison governor, a carefully-staged escape had been arranged.

Tomcat's apathy had been making the guards careless anyway. He kept up the appearance of being ill for a few more days, until the details of their release had been agreed on. When the escape over the wooden yard barricade happened, the rumour was quickly spread that he'd been pretending all along. By the time a search was sent out, Tomcat and Irish were both mounted on the horses waiting for them, and many miles away.

Tomcat reached out to stroke his horse's neck.

'Them lawmen sure did us well with these horses, didn't they?' he drawled.

Their own horses had been seized and sold on their imprisonment with a promise of the money being returned on release. Sheriff Darrow had used that money to get new mounts ready for them following their 'escape'. Judging by the quality of the new horses, he had spent some cash of his own too. Tomcat's new horse was a dun mare, with a neat white star and one white sock. She was sturdy, but there was good breeding in her head and she moved well. Tomcat had celebrated his release by naming her Liberty. Irish rode a tall, weight-carrying dark bay gelding with a crooked stripe down his face. Chinook wasn't a pretty horse, having a Roman nose, but he had plenty of solid bone and stamina.

'That they did,' Irish agreed. 'I guess he wants us to keep up with Captain Tom. He's always having good horses.'

'It's sure good to be toting our own weapons too,' Tomcat added.

'We got pretty much everything we need to be doing whatever we want,' Irish said.

The two men looked at one another for a few moments. Tomcat broke the silence.

'Where do you reckon Croucher's at?'

Irish shrugged. 'Could be Lucasville, Central or Golden. Or he could have upped and moved into the San Juans.'

'Or quit Colorado entirely,' Tomcat finished. 'I reckon Lucasville's the nearest place we can hear word about him.'

Irish nodded. 'We'll be after starting there then.'

Tomcat grinned suddenly. 'Then let's get a hustle on!' He shook up his reins and the dun mare leaped forward into a gallop.

Irish followed, smiling as the sound of Tomcat's laughter floated back to him on the wind.

★　★　★

'Two beers, and that bottle of rotgut.' Tomcat pointed at the one he wanted.

The barkeep fetched two glasses from under the counter and began pouring beer from a pitcher. 'You sure about that one?' he asked, pointing an elbow in the direction of the whiskey bottle. 'It ain't but half-full.'

'Then I only pay half price for it,' Tomcat answered.

When the drinks were served and paid for, Irish picked up one beer, while Tomcat took the other and the bottle of whiskey. Tomcat led the way across the half-full saloon, one of several that had sprung up almost overnight in the new boomtown of Leadville. There were busy games of faro and keno in one corner, while on a low platform opposite, two brightly-dressed women jigged half-heartedly to the music of a cheap piano. Other girls danced with customers or sweet-talked the men into buying them overpriced drinks.

For once, Tomcat paid no attention to the women. His attention was on a group of four men at a table near the centre of the room. Reaching them, he leaned over and deliberately placed the half-empty bottle in front of a tallish man with collar-length black hair. The conversation stopped. The black-haired man looked at the bottle, then at Tomcat. He had a long face, cut across with strong brows, and sharp, pale blue eyes. Thick, black hair swept across his forehead in a wave and brushed his collar at the back of his neck.

'A gift for you, Cap'n Croucher,' Tomcat drawled. His posture was relaxed but alert.

'A gift,' Tom Croucher repeated, picking up the bottle in his left hand. 'Looks like half a gift to me.'

Tomcat shrugged. 'You didn't do but half the job. You near 'bout killed that damn Sheriff Darrow but you didn't quite finish him. I'd sure enough like to see him dead but I don't care too hard iffen you didn't do it. I got a hankering to plug him myself.'

Croucher looked from Tomcat to Irish, standing behind him, and thought for a few moments. 'It's Tomcat Billy and Irish, ain't it?' Tomcat nodded. 'You and Black Elliot and some crazy Mex stole some jewellery in Darrow's town last summer. Made a damn big fuss at the time.'

'That's right,' Tomcat said.

Croucher stared at him. 'If I recall right, the other two was killed and you two were locked up?'

Tomcat grinned. 'You do remember right.' He recounted the prepared story of their 'escape', telling it well and with plenty of detail.

Tomcat studied Croucher as he spoke, without being too obvious. If they blew this chance to join the outlaw, they might never get another. From reaching Lucasville, it has taken just over a week of asking questions and following Croucher's trail across Colorado to reach him here, in Leadville. Tomcat could feel his heart pounding fast in his chest as he tried to convince the notorious outlaw of his escape, but he turned his anxiety into anger at Sheriff Darrow. Croucher wore a slight frown as Tomcat told his story, only smiling once. The three men with him all seemed to enjoy the tale more, which partially reassured Tomcat.

When he finished, Croucher nodded once. He looked thoughtfully at both Tomcat and Irish, his sharp blue eyes examining them.

'What are you aiming to do now?' Croucher asked.

'Pay Darrow back for putting me behind bars, and for killing Black Elliot and Curly Joe,' Tomcat said decisively.

Croucher took a gold watch from his jacket pocket and held it cupped in his hands, without opening the case to see the dial. He looked at it thoughtfully, rolling the heavy gold chain between his fingers. After a few moments, he turned to the man sitting beside him. 'Gemmill, get a half dozen shot glasses.'

Gemmill rose and headed for the bar. He was as big as Irish, but his features were rough-hewn and gave him a coarse, thuggish look. The beer glass at his place held nothing but plain water, for he was a strict teetotaller. Without waiting to be asked, Tomcat pulled out a chair and seated himself opposite Croucher. Irish snagged a free chair from the next table and settled down too. Fenner, a boyish-looking young man who sported a double gunbelt, scowled but didn't say anything.

When Gemmill returned with the glasses, Croucher poured shots from the bottle Tomcat had given him. Tomcat, Irish, Fenner and Croucher's other man, Jackson, all took their glasses. Gemmill picked up his water. Croucher raised his glass and looked at Tomcat.

'To Sheriff Darrow. May his life be short, and his death long and painful.'

The toast was echoed and the whiskey drunk. The liquor burned down Tomcat's throat to his stomach. Anxiety and excitement buzzed within him and made his green eyes glow with a wild light as he looked across the table to Croucher. The outlaw leader had made up his mind.

'I could use a couple more men. If you ride with me, we've got a better chance of getting Darrow together, than of getting him separately,' Croucher said. 'But I'm the captain. You do what I say.'

'So long as we're riding with you, that's a deal.' Tomcat held out his hand.

Croucher shook his hand, and then Irish's.

Fenner snorted and turned to face Tomcat. His youthful face was spoilt with a scornful look.

'We don't need this runt and his ox,' he sneered.

Tomcat immediately hooked his foot behind the front leg of Fenner's chair and pulled it sharply forward and up.

Taken by surprise, Fenner tumbled backward from his tilted chair and sprawled on the floor. Jackson, Gemmill and Irish laughed, as did others seated nearby. Croucher said nothing but watched with his usual slight frown as Fenner scrambled to his feet.

Tomcat had never taken his eyes from the other man. As he expected, Fenner came up with his fists bunched and swinging. Tomcat jumped to his feet and ducked neatly aside as Fenner swung at him. Grinning, he dodged another blow and nipped past Fenner, tipping the other man's hat off as he went. Fenner yelled and turned but Tomcat truly seemed as quick and agile as his namesake.

Fenner lashed out with both fists, the blows sharper and more controlled this time. Tomcat danced lightly from side to side, the punches never close enough to worry him. Fenner's tanned face was flushed with frustration. He feinted with his fist, then kicked out, aiming for Tomcat's knee. Tomcat swayed away from the punch but kept his balance well enough to jump clear of the kick. Landing on his toes, Tomcat bounded forward and past Fenner again, this time getting in a solid punch to Fenner's stomach.

Grunting, Fenner lashed out backwards, forcing Tomcat to duck deeper than intended. Fenner spun, meaning to kick again, but Tomcat had already recovered enough to leap lightly on to the seat of his chair. Fenner grabbed for the chair as Tomcat jumped down on the other side. He hurled the chair at Tomcat, then charged for the open space Tomcat would have to dodge into.

Tomcat chose to go the other way. He made a standing leap from the floor on to the table, not touching a single one of the glasses dotted about its surface. The chair flew through the place he'd been, heading now for Irish, who simply caught it in mid-air. Tomcat sketched a bow to Croucher, then jumped back off the table, twisting as he leapt, to land facing Fenner. He landed well, but as he began to recover and move, the toe of his moccasin caught against an unevenly laid floorboard. Not yet fully recovered from his illness in jail, Tomcat's strength and reflexes suddenly failed him. He was already slightly off-balance with the momentum of the jump, and simply fell flat, briefly winding himself.

Fenner gave a cry of triumph and moved, drawing his leg back to kick his enemy. Irish's chair scraped on the floor as he started to rise.

'Fenner! Enough!' Captain Croucher's command cut through the noise in the saloon.

Fenner paused, looking at Croucher with a sulky expression.

'He made a damned fool of me,' he protested.

'You wouldn't look a fool if you weren't one already,' Croucher told him. 'You know the rules. I don't tolerate my men fighting amongst themselves. Tomcat and Irish are my men now.'

Irish had moved over to his friend,

but let him get up on his own. Both knew that it was important for them to prove that they could look after themselves, especially the shorter and wiry Tomcat. Tomcat picked himself up, brushing dirt and sawdust from his brown jacket, and sat down again.

'Sorry 'bout that,' he drawled to Croucher.

Croucher sipped his whiskey. 'Got yourself someplace to stay here?' When Tomcat shook his head, Croucher jerked his thumb in the direction of the bar. 'Tell Sam there to find you two a room here: my request.'

Tomcat smiled. 'I surely appreciate that, Cap'n.' He nodded at the other man and rose to make for the bar.

7

Irish sat on his brass-framed bed and looked about the room. There were calico curtains at the window, a little sun-faded and drooping at the hem, but clean. The beds had patterned, calico-covered quilts over fat, straw mattresses that crackled when he moved. Tomcat paced restlessly between the two beds, before hauling up the window and sitting on the sill, leaning against the frame. He peered out into the dark street below, then tilted his head to look up at the stars.

'Sure an' this ain't no prison cell,' Irish remarked.

Tomcat sighed, and turned to look in at his friend. 'I know. But this'll be the first time I slept indoors since we got out of the hogpen.' He shook his head briskly, as though trying to clear it.

Irish studied him, his pale blue eyes revealing little of his thoughts.

'Now we're after finding Croucher, we can wire Darrow in the morning,' he said eventually. 'Once he's got Croucher, we can be doing what we please.'

'I'm out of jail,' Tomcat replied, still gazing outwards. 'I can do whatever I've got a mind to, and I ain't minded to please Sheriff Darrow.'

Irish didn't answer that, just traced the pattern on the quilt with his broad finger.

Tomcat sat silently for a few moments, then swung his legs over the window sill so they hung outside the building. 'I'm goin' out. Don't know when I'll be back.' As Irish nodded acknowledgement, Tomcat slipped out of the window and vanished.

Irish didn't bother looking out to see him climb down. Climbing the outside of a building was no harder for Tomcat than climbing a flight of stairs was for most people. He stretched out on his bed, thinking about the encounter with Croucher and his men. The outlaw leader made Irish feel very uncomfortable; every instinct warned him to stay away.

Tomcat's moodiness also bothered him. Irish had been reconsidering things since the lawmen had made their remarkable offer a couple of weeks ago. After leaving home nearly ten years ago, he'd drifted from occasional petty crime into becoming a full-time bank robber and outlaw. Most of it had been pretty good times, especially after meeting Tomcat a few years back. They'd shared rooms, food and even women, living from one day to the next. And all Irish had to show for his time was the memories. Even Croucher, an outlaw for longer, had little more than he could carry in his saddle-bags. It didn't seem much of a return for the danger and hardships.

Aside from Tomcat, Irish had never met another outlaw he really trusted, and he was pretty sure most of those he'd met didn't trust him either. The strange thing was that he trusted the two lawmen, Darrow and Keating. Both were from completely different worlds to his; they were gentlemen, educated and wealthy. Irish was sure that Darrow was only trusting him because he had no choice, but he was certain that if he and Tomcat did succeed in helping the lawman capture Croucher, then Darrow would keep his promise to have them both pardoned.

By some miracle, they'd been given a second chance, and Irish intended to take it. If Tomcat refused to go straight, Irish would have to make a tough decision about their friendship. He shied away from thinking about that, and lay on his bed, thinking hard about what else they might do with their lives.

★   ★   ★

Tomcat and Irish were both up and half-dressed the next morning when there was an abrupt knock on the door. It opened before either replied, and Jackson stuck his head around.

'There's grub ready downstairs,' he informed them. 'Hurry and get some afore we rides out.'

He withdrew rapidly in a flurry of wild, red hair, and slammed the door.

There was no time for a visit to the telegraph office to wire Darrow. Barely half an hour later, Tomcat and Irish were riding out of Leadville with Tom Croucher and his gang. No one told them where they were going. They headed east, following a gulch that led to a pass over the Mosquito Range. It was still early and the day was fresh as the horses climbed the trail, leaving the smoke and noise of the town behind them. Irish couldn't help enjoying the ride, in spite of his reservations about what they were doing. Tomcat Billy had no such reservations: he began singing his favourite song.

'In a cavern, in a canyon, excavating for a mine, dwelt a miner, forty-niner, and his daughter . . . '

'Shut the hell up!' yelled Fenner, turning round in his saddle to glare at Tomcat.

'Let him sing,' Gemmill insisted. 'Tomcat's got a fine voice. I sure like to hear someone who can sing, which is more'n you-all kin do.'

'Why thank you,' Tomcat drawled, smiling at Gemmill.

Fenner looked at Croucher. The outlaw leader merely stared flatly at him for a few moments, then turned away. Tomcat started to sing again, relaxed into his saddle. Fenner bumped his heels against his bay's sides, jogging her to the front of the group and away from Tomcat.

Fenner's mood was much the same by the time they stopped to make camp for the night. However, Jackson and Gemmill had both talked some to the newcomers. Croucher made camp a little way off the trail. He still hadn't told his new recruits where they were headed, but Irish could see the smoke of a town a few miles distant. Since crossing the ridge, they had ridden down into the head of a wide, flattish grassy valley ringed with towering mountains: one of Colorado's natural parks.

'I'm after thinking that might be Fairplay,' Irish said to Tomcat as they saw to their horses.

Tomcat quickly ran the hoofpick around the sole of his mare's near forefoot, then released the hoof. He straightened, patting the horse's neck, as he turned his eyes to the smoke rising in the distance. 'I guess you're right. Reckon we're gonna make a visit tomorrow? A mining town like that's gonna have a couple a ripe banks waiting to be plucked.'

Irish spoke quietly, his voice deepening to a rumble. 'Sure and I wish Croucher hadn't brought us out on a job so soon. I wanted to get this over without doing a raid with him.'

Tomcat's green eyes sparkled. 'If we go along with a raid or two before we report back, we can earn ourselves some cash-money with our shares. Then we'll have something to start over with, after.'

Irish felt cold inside. 'Let's go get some of that coffee that's brewing,' he said abruptly, and moved away.

Tomcat followed, whistling.

*   *   *

As they broke camp the next morning, Croucher came over to Tomcat and Irish. They watched as he inspected their horses, checking that the tack was in good repair and fitted properly, and examining the horses' legs and hoofs. Tomcat fidgeted as he watched, impatience sparking in his green eyes. A man's mount was his own responsibility, and Croucher's inspection suggested a lack of faith in his new companions. Irish frowned at his friend, and Tomcat managed to hold silence until Croucher was done.

'Do we have to parade for inspection every morning?' Tomcat asked tartly.

Croucher's long face was cold and unrevealing. 'We ride far and we ride fast. You need good horses in good condition. I needed to see how you look after your mounts before I let you go any further with us.' He glanced briefly at Irish before turning his attention back to Tomcat. 'If your horse can't keep up because of something that's your fault, I'll leave you behind.'

'I know how to handle horses,' Tomcat asserted.

Croucher nodded. 'These two are fine.'

'So where are we riding to?' Tomcat asked.

'Fairplay.' Croucher nodded in the direction of the smoke rising into the sky. 'There's a couple of banks there. We're going for the South Park National Bank. I want you two to stay outside as lookouts. Anyone starts taking notice of what's happening, anyone gets the idea to be a hero and stop us, you dissuade them. Scare 'em off, shoot them iffen you have to.'

Tomcat nodded. 'We're with you, Cap'n.'

Irish just nodded; he couldn't quite bring himself to verbally commit to Tom Croucher and his gang. He kept his expression blank, giving the impression of a docile ox, willing to obey orders. Croucher did no more than glance at the big, quiet man, and head back to his own horse.

★　★　★

Irish's bay gelding stretched out its neck and shook itself before settling down again, its hips cocked as it rested one back leg. Irish half wished that he could be so relaxed, instead of having this churning feeling in his stomach. He'd not felt like this since his first robbery but then he'd been excited, as well as nervous. Now, he just wanted the whole business to be safely over and done. He turned in his saddle and looked along the quiet street to where Tomcat was stationed. Tomcat's attention was on a gaudily-dressed woman walking along the other side of the street.

South Park National Bank was on a corner near the centre of the small town. At mid-morning, the streets were pretty quiet. There was no sound of anything untoward from the bank, even though Croucher and the rest of his men had gone in nearly five minutes earlier. So far no one else had tried to enter the bank, but Irish had a strong feeling of time running out. He looked about again, watching the woman for a few moments as she flaunted past. His interest was entirely focussed on her potential as a danger.

Satisfied that she wasn't interested in the bank, or the two men sitting on their horses in the street, Irish turned and looked back down the other street the bank faced on to. He tensed as he saw a man in a grey town suit walk along and glance in through the bank windows. The man's pace slowed, then he abruptly changed direction and sprinted back the way he'd come. Cursing under his breath, Irish snatched off his black hat and swung it in the air. Tomcat caught the signal and pressed his horse into a run, as Irish was doing the same.

Hat jammed back on over his fair hair, Irish aimed his horse down the street after the witness. The big, raw-boned bay took a few strides to get up to speed. The man Irish was chasing turned into a hardware store just past the bank, without realizing that Irish was after him. As Irish got closer to the bank, he too glanced through the windows and saw a couple of customers and a guard standing in a line with their hands in the air.

Though slow to start, the bay's long stride covered the ground fast. Irish brought the horse to a sliding halt outside the hardware store, kicking up a cloud of dirt. As he turned in the saddle, the door of the store was hauled open. Irish glimpsed the double barrels coming through first, and grabbed for his pistol. He got the gun pointed at the doorway just as the grey-suited man came into view behind his shotgun. The witness stopped dead, the shotgun pointed down and to one side.

'Stop!' Irish yelled, cocking the

hammer of his plain Peacemaker. 'Get back inside.'

The witness was a young man, no older than Irish. He wore a decent suit, but the hands holding the shotgun were strong, labourer's hands. He scowled at Irish and whipped up the shotgun. Faced with such a deadly weapon, Irish was forced to shoot. He deliberately aimed a little to one side; his bullet tore a chunk from the doorframe by the witness's shoulder. The man flinched, then began to ready the shotgun again. Irish hastily changed his aim and fired. The witness screamed as the bullet tore through his left leg. His body jerked and the barrels of the shotgun swung high and wide as he accidentally pulled the trigger. Irish felt the shot pass his head at close range, but the man was falling backwards into the doorway of the store.

Irish played on the reins as the bay snorted and plunged. Turning the horse, he kicked it into a gallop back the way he'd come. A quick glance back over his shoulder reassured him that the man he'd just shot was still moving. The sickness in his stomach subsided a little but his heart was still pounding like an overworked steam engine.

Tomcat appeared round the corner of the bank, pistol in hand, and looking ready to fight. He saw Irish heading his way and the fierce look changed to a big grin. He gave a whoop of excitement then turned in his saddle, checking his surroundings. Irish glimpsed movement in a shop window and fired towards it. No glass broke, so he felt sure he hadn't hit anyone. He just wanted the citizens to stay inside and out of the way.

Rounding the corner after Tomcat, Irish saw Croucher and his gang leaping into the saddles of their horses. Croucher's bay had a gunny sack fastened to the saddle now; it was supposed to contain the loot from the bank but looked almost empty. Fenner yelled as he spurred his horse forward, and fired shots into the doorway of a saloon opposite. They raced up the street together, Croucher and Fenner firing shots as they went. Irish holstered his gun and concentrated on riding. From what he could see, Croucher was a more focussed version of his usual self, the strong brows down over cold blue eyes, his habitual frown deepened. Fenner was slightly flushed with excitement, his rounded face like that of a schoolboy let out of school early. Except Fenner had moved from pulling the wings off flies to shooting at anyone who showed his head.

8

Fortunately, no one attempted to stop the robbers as they fled Fairplay. They galloped fast for a mile, then Croucher slowed the pace to a mile-eating jog that the horses could keep up for hours. Tomcat reined his dun alongside Irish's horse. His green eyes were still bright but he was more relaxed now, moving easily in his saddle.

He looked Irish up and down as they rode.

'I heard a shotgun; you didn't get hit anywheres?' he drawled.

Irish shook his head. 'Not so much as a pellet. Sure an' I was lucky.' He shuddered at the memory of the near-miss.

Tomcat looked at him thoughtfully. 'You shot the feller?'

'In the leg. He was still moving so I'll be hoping he pulls through.'

Tomcat made an agreeing sound.

'Reckon I hope so too.' He brightened up, an irrepressible grin breaking out. Tomcat took a deep breath of the fresh mountain air, his eyes darting about as he took in the beauty of the wide grassy meadow, ringed by snow-touched peaks. 'Goddam it, Irish, this is sure 'nuff like heaven. I can't remember the last time I felt so alive.'

'It's a shame you ain't dead,' Fenner interrupted, holding up his horse so Tomcat and Irish caught up. 'You two was supposed to be lookouts and you couldn't even get that right.'

'I done warned you there was trouble, didn't I?' Tomcat flung back. 'If we'd tried to stop folks walking along the street, that would have tipped them off as sure as God made little green apples, you son-of-a-bitch.'

'Why, you short-assed runt!' Fenner yanked his horse sideways, trying to barge it into Tomcat's.

The dun spun nimbly, dodging the other horse. The other riders came to a disorganized halt.

'Drop it, both of you!' Croucher commanded. He urged his horse between them, forcing Tomcat and Fenner apart. The cold blue stare swept each man in turn. 'This ain't the place to argue. We got to keep moving.' He stared at Fenner. 'Any chewing out is my job. I tell folk iffen they done good or bad.' The piercing eyes turned on Tomcat. 'I'll talk to you and Irish when we stop. I want to know exactly what happened back there. Got it?'

Tomcat nodded, still angry, but willing to accept Croucher's authority.

Croucher glanced at Fenner again. 'Come on.' He eased his horse into a lope and the others followed in silence.

★　★　★

'I know it's been nearly three weeks,' Hugh Keating said crossly. 'But Colorado's a big territory. You can't expect them to find Croucher just like that.'

Pacey folded his arms and looked down at his fellow deputy. 'Colorado's

113

not a territory anymore; it became a state last year.'

Hugh's first response was a word he wouldn't have used in front of Minnie. However, they were in the law office, getting ready to do the Saturday evening patrol around town.

'They've behaved like the scum they are, and headed for tall timber,' Pacey said. He moved away from the desk he'd been leaning against and started to circle Hugh. 'I bet they're on their way to California now, or maybe even Mexico. Two more criminals on the loose, and it was your idea to let them out. Your idea to take the word of two outlaws, known thieves.'

Hugh turned awkwardly on the spot to keep Pacey in sight as the other man walked slowly around him. 'All right, so it was my idea. But Darrow went along with it, and so did the governor of the jail. You didn't come up with any better ideas,' he added accusingly.

'I couldn't have come up with a worse one!'

Hugh was starting to feel dizzy from turning round and round. He halted, swaying slightly, and glared at the taller and younger man. 'I . . . '

His opinion was interrupted by the arrival of the sheriff. Darrow stalked in from the street, his saturnine face hard. The emotion was in his dark eyes, which scorched Hugh as the sheriff approached him. Darrow thrust the newspaper he was carrying into Hugh's chest, almost into his face. Hugh instinctively grabbed the paper, recoiling from the sheriff's expression. There was a silence before Darrow spoke, low and fierce.

'I was a fool to listen to you.'

Hugh just blinked at him.

'What's happened?' Pacey reached for the newspaper that Hugh was clutching.

Hugh jerked it away from him, scowling, then turned the paper so he could read it.

'This is a Denver paper,' he said. His eyes darted over the printing, then widened. 'Croucher has robbed a bank!'

'So much for bringing him to justice,' Pacey said, trying to read over his shoulder.

'It gets better,' Darrow drawled.

'It says there were six men in the gang,' Hugh read. 'A passer-by saw the people in the bank with their hands raised, and went to raise the alarm. One of the gang's lookouts shot him. The lookout was a large man with a fair goatee, riding a big, Roman-nosed bay with a crooked stripe.' Hugh looked up. 'That's Irish!'

Pacey reached over his shoulder to point at another paragraph. 'There was another lookout — a slight fellow wearing moccasins and riding a dun mare; Tomcat Billy!' He slapped Hugh on the shoulder. 'See? I said all along that pair couldn't be trusted. They've found Croucher all right, and now they're riding with him!'

Hugh looked up, caught the sheriff's expression, and paled slightly. All the same, he shook his head. 'I don't think they are. Well, they are. They're with Croucher, but they're not *with* him.' Aware that he was babbling, Hugh waved a hand as he tried to explain. 'I mean, they took part in this robbery but it doesn't make sense if they want to go back on their word and not help us.

'If all Tomcat and Irish wanted to do was simply run — break the deal and get where we'd never find them — then they'd just vanish. They'd go to California, or leave the country. Riding with Captain Croucher means they're bound to be seen and reported.'

'So they want revenge,' Pacey said. 'They want revenge on us for arresting them. Croucher wants revenge for his brother's death. Makes sense for them to team up.'

'If they were going to team up, would they make it so obvious?' Hugh asked.

'They're criminals; they're don't have the sense God gave geese,' Pacey retorted. 'And whatever the reason, the fact is, Irish shot someone, and all for

117

just two hundred and thirty dollars.'

Hugh looked at the paper again. 'Two hundred and thirty? That's not very much.'

Darrow showed his teeth in a humourless smile. 'That's the only passel of good news in this mess. Croucher for sure picked the wrong day to go to the bank. He went just after payday, after the money had gone out to the mines, and before the miners could get into town to spend it.'

'It just serves those lying no-goods right,' Pacey said. 'They got themselves on the wrong side of the law again, and all for less than forty dollars apiece. You'd best telegraph the sheriffs down in Colorado and tell them to go ahead and arrest Tomcat and Irish the minute they set eyes on them,' he told Darrow.

'I don't think it's as bad as it seems,' Hugh said stubbornly. He looked at Darrow. 'You've got to trust them a little longer.'

The sheriff hesitated a moment before speaking. His gaze lost focus briefly, then sharpened on Hugh. 'I don't trust anyone,' he said flatly. 'Come on; it's time we made the first patrol.' He turned and left the office as abruptly as he'd arrived.

Hugh snatched up his hat and hurried after him. There was an uneasy feeling in the pit of his stomach. For just a few moments, he'd seen Sheriff Darrow doubt himself. They'd been working together for several years now, but such a thing was so rare, it had taken Hugh a few moments to realize what he was seeing in Darrow's eyes.

Darrow set off at a brisk pace, down Main Street to the railroad, then back up Lincoln Street. Hugh knew that Darrow still wasn't fit, but a restless anger gave him energy. As they reached the junction with Cross Street, they heard yells. Darrow turned his head to listen for a moment, then broke into a run. Hugh followed, holding the shotgun in both hands.

'The White Buffalo?' he panted.

Darrow didn't bother to answer; he

just turned the corner into Judd Street.

The saloon had doors and windows open on this pleasant June evening. The music of an automatic piano was almost drowned by a series of yells and whoops, punctuated by sporadic crashes. Hugh was glad not to hear gunfire, but held his shotgun a little tighter anyway. Darrow led the way into the saloon, pausing slightly as his eyes adjusted to the lower light level. The busy room smelt sharply of tobacco, sweat and beer. The trouble was coming from a table closer to the small dance floor. A drunken cowhand was standing on it, being cheered on by his friends, and cheerfully lobbing glasses and bottles at random targets about the room. Some of the other saloon-goers were yelling for him to stop and others were pointing out targets for him. One of the bar staff was being held in place by two cowhands as he yelled furiously at the bottle thrower.

The sheriff didn't bother shouting orders. He squared his shoulders and barged his way through the gathering crowd. A red-faced cowhand he knocked aside raised his hands as though to grab Darrow's collar.

'Forget it!' Hugh snapped, hefting the shotgun and hoping he didn't look too frightened.

The cowhand saw the shotgun, and then Hugh's badge, and backed off. Others scattered as they realized the law had arrived.

The cowhand on the table saw the ripple of movement in the crowd, and turned to look. He gave a whoop, waving a bottle in the air.

'Say, it's the sheriff, done come to join the party!'

'The sheriff's hat!' someone in the crowd yelled.

The cowhand whooped again, and drew back his arm to throw the bottle.

Darrow dived forwards and the bottle sailed over his head. Hugh ducked neatly out of the way, wincing as he heard the bottle hit someone behind him. Ahead, Darrow grabbed the edge of the table and heaved upwards. There was a yell and some frantic arm-waving, as the cowhand fell in a scatter of coins, glasses and cigarette butts. The table went over on its side, the cowhand hitting the floorboards beside it. Darrow didn't pause, but leapt around the table.

He was on the cowhand before the other man could do anything more than groan breathlessly. Darrow struck him hard across the side of his head with the butt of his gun. The cowhand grunted in pain, and tried to roll away. Darrow raised his arm again; Hugh lunged forward and caught his wrist. He was almost pulled off-balance as the sheriff tried to strike but saved himself with an undignified lurch.

'Darrow, enough!' Fear for his friend loaned him unaccustomed authority as he spoke.

Darrow turned, his eyes burning with anger. After a silent moment, he blinked, recognizing Hugh. The sheriff stayed as he was briefly, gathering together his self-control. His face became inscrutable, but his eyes betrayed a hint of stronger emotions held tightly within. Darrow twisted his wrist free of Hugh's grip, and rose. He gestured for a couple of the cowhands standing by to see to their semi-conscious friend. One immediately bent over the groaning man. The other stared sullenly at Darrow before turning to help. Someone else set the table upright again and began to gather the debris. With the excitement over, the gathered crowd began to break up as people drifted back to their own tables, talking about the incident.

Hugh made a vague apology to the injured drunk and his friends, then hurried after Darrow as the sheriff made his way outside. The warm evening air seemed much fresher, carrying a faint scent of woodsmoke and the inevitable slight tang of horse dung. Hugh took a deep breath, clearing away the smells of stale beer, bodies and tobacco, then joined Darrow, who was leaning with his forearms on the hitching rail. Darrow continued to stare across the street at the office of the town's newspaper, ignoring his deputy.

Even when bending forward, his posture was still rigid.

Hugh leaned more casually, a less imposing figure. He stood in silence for a minute, studying the sheriff's saturnine face.

'You really find it hard to trust other people, don't you?' he remarked eventually.

Darrow didn't reply.

'Tomcat and Irish are your best chance of getting Captain Croucher and you don't think they'll do it,' Hugh went on. 'Not just because they're criminals. You wouldn't be bothered much about that if you were there with them. It's because you can't be there. You just don't trust them to get the job done without you.'

Darrow stirred slightly. 'If not for the war, I would have been a lawyer. Do you think either Tomcat or Irish are intelligent enough to become a lawyer?'

'They'd have more sense than to try,' Hugh retorted. 'Though they're both criminal enough to be successful at it.'

Darrow showed his teeth in a dry smile. 'Point taken.' The smile vanished. 'A friend once told me that a man who trusts can never be betrayed, only mistaken. I hate to make mistakes.'

'Nobody's perfect,' Hugh replied. 'Not even you.'

Darrow turned and looked at Hugh. After a pause, he said, 'Thank you,' his gaze flickering back towards the saloon. With that, he straightened and turned. 'Come on, we've got the rest of the patrol to do.'

★   ★   ★

The next morning, a telegram was delivered to the sheriff's office:

In central stop suggest you use taxes to bait trap your side of line stop irish

Darrow's eyes brightened as he read the message, but all he said was: 'The odds have shortened.'

125

9

Irish fiddled with a lock of his horse's mane, unable to concentrate on anything much other than a sound he couldn't yet hear. He, Tomcat, Croucher and Jackson were bunched together in a gulch off the main trail from Central City down to Denver. Fenner and Gemmill were concealed someone on the other side of the trail. Very soon now, a stagecoach carrying passengers and gold would pass this way. Croucher's face was more intense than usual as he waited, listening for the approach of the stage.

Croucher and his men had already been low on cash before the Fairplay bank raid, and the money from that hadn't gone far between six men and their horses. Both Jackson's and Gemmill's horses had needed shoeing in Central; Jackson had been forced to sell a few of his books to help pay for both. Croucher had his gold watch but Irish guessed it had sentimental value, as Croucher often looked at it without opening it to read the time. There was no question of selling it, anyway.

A moment later, Irish heard it: the pounding of hoofs and the rattling of coach and harness. Their horses lifted their heads and pricked their ears. The riders pulled bandannas up to cover their faces and drew pistols. Irish's bay caught the sudden air of tension and pawed the ground. Croucher looked around swiftly at the men with him, then nodded.

They swept out on to the trail together. The stage was closer than Irish had thought, the six-horse team coming towards them at a steady lope. The guard started to raise his rifle, then hesitated. The driver was more determined; he lifted his whip, preparing to urge his team forward, running the gauntlet of the ambush. The outlaws steadied their horses, ready to swing out of its path, even as guns were raised. Then Fenner and Gemmill burst out from their cover on the other side of the trail. Fenner whooped, and fired his gun in the air. The nearest team horse shied away from the gunshot, pushing against its mate. The team broke stride and lost momentum.

'Hold it!' Croucher yelled, aiming his pistol straight at the driver.

The stagecoach driver tightened the lines, playing the multiple sets of reins with one hand while holding the whip with the other. The guard's hands twitched, then stilled, keeping the muzzle of his Winchester pointing towards the sky as he glared at the outlaws. The team dropped to a trot, and halted in very few paces.

'Drop your weapons, slowly,' Croucher barked.

The guard leaned over, holding his rifle by the barrel, and lowered it from the seat before letting it drop to the ground. The driver put up his whip, pulled the brake on, and then dropped a pistol into the dirt.

'Down.' Croucher gestured sharply with his gun.

The outlaws began moving before anyone on the coach could get themselves organized. Tomcat, Jackson and Gemmill passed their reins to Irish and headed to the stagecoach. Croucher and Fenner positioned themselves either side of the team and kept the guard and driver covered as they climbed down. Gemmill yanked the door of the coach open.

'Out,' he growled succinctly. The gesture of his big Colt added emphasis.

As the passengers began to climb out, under Gemmill's and Jackson's guns, Tomcat picked up the driver's pistol and tucked it into the waist of his trousers. Springing on to the wheel, he neatly ascended the stagecoach. Tomcat barely seemed to make contact with the wood as he flew swiftly from ground to the driver's box. The first passenger had barely set foot on the trail before Tomcat had the leather boot under the seat open. Jackson pulled out a small gunny sack and held it for the passengers to drop their valuables into.

'Got it.' Tomcat began to heave at something in the front boot.

Irish watched him struggling to move a heavy chest and fought down the urge to go and help him. He looked to Croucher, wondering who he'd send to help Tomcat; it would surely have to wait until Gemmill and Jackson had finished with the half dozen passengers. Tomcat grunted as he heaved at the wooden strongbox, struggling to get it on to the footrest at the front of the boot. Irish glanced at the sullen passengers, then turned his attention back to Tomcat's efforts.

The crash of a gunshot made Irish jump. The horses snorted and one plunged, almost pulling its reins from his hand. Tomcat was startled too. He lost his grip on the strongbox, which slipped from the footrest. It hit the trail dirt with a thud and metallic crash. The wood split in two places and bright, golden ingots spilled into the dust. Croucher swore, standing in his stirrups to see what had happened. Fenner was just visible on the other side, his boyish face bright with excitement.

'He drew on me!' Fenner exclaimed.

Irish leaned low in his saddle and saw the body of the stage guard crumpled near the front wheel on the far side. A moment later, Tomcat landed beside the guard and bent down to examine the body. The stage driver was cursing in a steady monotone, his eyes glaring hate at Croucher.

'Dead,' Tomcat called, straightening up. 'Plugged him plumb between the eyes.'

Croucher turned on the driver. 'You! Shut the hell up!' He continued to shout instructions as his horse sidled restlessly. 'Fenner, help Tomcat. Gemmill, deal with those passengers and get them back inside.' He glanced over his shoulder at Irish; his blue eyes were bright and his body tense, as though ready to lash out. 'Bring the horses in closer,' he snapped.

Irish obeyed, unfastening the saddle-bags he could reach. Fenner dismounted, leaving his horse ground-tied. He hammered the splintered strongbox with the butt of his pistol, breaking it further. More gold slid out, scattering almost under the rear hoofs of the wheeler horses. Tomcat grabbed a couple of the small ingots and ducked through, underneath the stagecoach, to reach Irish. He packed the ingots quickly into a saddle-bag, and turned back to Fenner. Fenner was picking up the scattered gold, muttering curses as the off-wheeler stamped its back leg, and swished its tail restlessly. Tomcat patted the near-wheeler horse on its quarters, speaking quietly to it, before reaching behind the two wheelers to take the ingots that Fenner passed to him from the other side.

There was a sudden cry of pain and something bumped heavily against the stage. It rocked and the near-wheeler horse kicked out, narrowly missing Tomcat's head.

One of the passengers, a youngish man, was slumped in the open door of the stage, blood trickling down his forehead. He moaned and pressed his hand against his face.

'Don't be so damn stupid,' Gemmill growled. He grabbed the man with one large hand and pushed him inside. 'Sit down and don't try anything else.'

Other passengers hauled the stunned man inside.

Irish went on soothing the restless horses. While Gemmill stayed to guard the passengers inside the coach, Jackson joined Tomcat and Fenner in loading gold into the saddle-bags. Picking the ingots up from around horses' hoofs made the process slower than anyone wanted. Fenner snapped at Tomcat once; the near horse swished its tail and stamped fretfully. Fenner glanced anxiously at it, then had the sense to keep his mouth shut. He shoved a pile of the ingots towards Tomcat, then started gathering nearer ones to put into the saddle-bags of his own horse.

'That's enough,' Croucher called at last.

There was still gold on the ground

and in the shattered strongbox but Irish didn't care. He just wanted to get away. First though, Tomcat, Gemmill and Fenner moved around the team, unhitching traces and loosening buckles. The horses weren't loose enough to get away, but the time taken for the driver to hitch the team properly again would delay the stage's journey further still and buy the outlaws more time to get away before a posse could be raised. At last, the outlaws vaulted into their saddles and departed at a brisk trot.

They rode north, bypassing Central City and climbing the ridge of snowy peaks beyond. Hard riding finally brought them into another of the wide, grassy parks that nestled among the mountains. When Croucher called a halt for the day, the weary horses were tended to first. The men were tired too, but the horses were watered, rubbed down, inspected and fed grain before the men so much as brewed coffee.

After they'd eaten, Irish went for a short stroll to loosen his muscles after a day in the saddle. He found himself wandering alongside the creek, just out of sight of the camp. The rippling of the water was soothing, so he sat down on the bank. Irish gazed at the shadowy fish in the creek as he thought.

A year and a half ago, he'd have been delighted by the gold now in his saddle-bags. There was enough to keep him comfortably for months, if not a year, without having to do a day's work. But this gold felt tainted.

'Irish?'

He started, turning to see Tomcat Billy standing beside him. Tomcat's smile was awkward, as though he wasn't sure if it was appropriate.

'Sit down,' Irish said impulsively.

Tomcat did so, gracefully. He gazed out over the creek for a few moments, absently pulling at the grass with one hand.

'The guard weren't armed,' he drawled, and paused. 'I looked an' he weren't carrying no pistol. Fenner . . . murdered him.'

Irish didn't say anything immediately. Tomcat threw some blades of grass at the creek and watched them float out of sight.

'I ain't goin' back inside!' he said with sudden vehemence. 'I won't. I can't!' The last word was almost a wail. Tomcat shuddered and took a sobbing gulp. He drew his legs up and wrapped his arms around himself, forcing himself to breathe steadily. Irish waited patiently until the haunted look left Tomcat's eyes and he began to relax. Tomcat began to speak again, his Tennessee drawl thicker than usual as the words poured out of him.

'Croucher and his gang have killed afore and now they done notched up another killin'. That slab-head fool used our names. The law'll sure enough be after him harder now. If we're with him when the law catches up to him, they ain't gonna care too hard who they throw in jail with him. I won't go back inside; I won't. I'd rather they done killed me than put me inside again.' He paused a moment, looking across the stream to the grassy meadow and the mountains beyond. 'I don't wanna die,' he finished softly.

'No more do I, I'm thinking,' Irish answered. He turned and looked straight at his friend. 'I don't want to die, and I surely don't want to be wasting my life in and out of jail. Sheriff Darrow's done give us a chance to start clean, and I aim to take it. I ain't gonna ride with Croucher, nor any other owlhoots. I'll stay with Croucher for so long as it takes the law to catch him an' that's it's for sure. That's my choice.'

He spoke firmly, knowing that he believed in what he said, but in his heart, Irish was nervous. If Tomcat refused to go straight, it would effectively mean the end of that friendship. Looking at his friend, sitting tensely beside him, Irish felt guilty at potentially abandoning him.

Tomcat stayed as he was, rocking back and forth gently. After a minute or so, he turned his green eyes on his friend. 'You managed to telegraph Sheriff Darrow?'

Irish nodded. 'Told him we was in Central. I was after thinking about how to get Darrow and Croucher up against one another. Darrow was out getting taxes when Croucher bushwhacked him, so I told Darrow he should make another trip like that.'

Tomcat grinned. 'You told Darrow to make himself bait in a trap?' He laughed sharply. 'I reckon he's that plumb mad at Croucher, he'd do it. After all, he got us out to help him, didn't he?'

'For sure an' he did,' Irish agreed. 'An' I went and gave him my word, and I intend keeping it. I'll side with Darrow iffen it comes to a fight with Croucher.'

Tomcat was silent a moment. 'I don't like Croucher's killing ways, but it was Darrow as put me in a cell. If we get them together, I don't care too hard which one dies. Whatever happens, I ain't goin' inside again.'

'The best way to stay out of jail is not to commit any crimes,' Irish said.

'Or not get caught,' Tomcat replied. He lifted his head to a shout from the camp. 'Sounds like supper's ready.' He rose gracefully and set off without looking back.

Supper that evening was salt pork and beans. The mood of the group was more relaxed than at any time since Tomcat and Irish had joined Croucher's band. After eating, they settled down. Jackson read a book, Gemmill mended a sock and Fenner simply lay on his stomach, building stacks with gold ingots as though they were a child's wooden building blocks. Irish was brushing dried sweat from his saddle blanket. Tomcat settled himself next to Croucher, who was sipping at a mug of strong, black tea.

'Where're we goin' next?' Tomcat asked.

Croucher looked sideways at him. 'Aren't satisfied with the gold you got today?'

Tomcat nodded. 'Sure I am! But it ain't the only thing I got a hankerin' for. I aim to see Sheriff Darrow dead, and I reckon as we should act now, while we got this gold.'

Croucher simply gave him an inquiring look.

'See, with this gold, once we kill Darrow, we can run as far as we want.' Tomcat's green eyes were bright. 'We can travel to California — hell, we could even go to New York. We can get wherever we like and the law won't find us.'

'Why not just take the gold and forget about Darrow?' Croucher asked, the sharp blue eyes searching Tomcat's face.

Tomcat met his gaze. 'It's pretty near on a year since Darrow sent me to the hogpen. I reckon that's plenty long enough for him to be livin' on. Killing him a year on seems pretty neat. 'Sides, you got a powerful reason to want him dead, don't you?'

Croucher took the watch from his

pocket and held it cupped in his hands. 'You know I haven't forgotten Dan,' he said softly. 'Darrow still owes me for his life.'

'You found him afore, didn't you? The sheriff's gotta give notice of when he's goin' to do things like collect taxes, or run a bankrupt auction. We find out where he's goin' and bushwhack him on his way there.'

Croucher stared at the watch's closed case. 'I promised Dan I'd put that sheriff in his grave. I aim to keep that promise.' He spoke mostly to himself.

Tomcat didn't press him any further, but retreated to join Irish.

10

Hugh held up his glass of whiskey, admiring the glow of the liquor in the beam of sunlight that cut through the office. Darrow suddenly whirled away from the window to the desk. He grabbed the whiskey bottle with one hand, and snatched Hugh's glass with the other.

'What?' Hugh sat upright in the office chair.

Darrow hastily stashed both items in the deep drawer at the bottom of the desk.

'Robinson. For god's sake, look smart,' the sheriff snapped.

Hugh grabbed his pen from the stand, and flipped open the log book. When the office door opened, Hugh was writing busily, while Darrow inspected one of the shotguns from the rack on the rear wall of the law office.

Justice Robinson entered, looking

suspiciously at the lawmen. The town's leading lawyer, and justice of the peace, he was a short man with a face like a roughly made currant bun, and dark hair, firmly oiled into place. Robinson had been one of the first inhabitants of Govan, and was an important figure on the town council. He disliked the taller, handsome Darrow, and despised Hugh. Advancing across the room, he tossed a copy of the *Govan Herald* on to the desk.

'One man dead and another injured. Nine thousand dollars of gold stolen. And your men were responsible.'

Darrow half-lifted one hand, pointing at Robinson. 'I've read the report too,' he said coldly. 'Tomcat and Irish were certainly there, but they weren't the ones doing the shooting.'

'They took part in that robbery,' Robinson returned. 'It was your idea to turn them loose again.'

Darrow's dark eyes glared. 'Yes. And everyone involved; myself, you, the Governor — we all knew that they were robbers. But they are not killers. Croucher and his original gang are the killers. Croucher's crimes go back years before he met Tomcat Billy and Irish. Getting someone in his gang to betray him could be our best chance of stopping Croucher and making him pay for everything he's done.'

'*If* they betray him,' Robinson said witheringly. '*If* they don't just decide they'd rather take their share of nine thousand dollars, and just vanish.'

'How do you expect Tomcat to get Croucher to trust them if they refuse to take part in his activities?' Darrow tilted his head slightly as he spoke. 'Surely you don't expect them to stay behind and darn their socks while Croucher robs banks?'

Robinson glared coldly back, unperturbed by having to look up at the taller sheriff.

'What I expect is for lawmen to lock up criminals, not to turn them loose,' he replied. 'I cannot believe that you are letting a pair of convicted men do your work for you.'

Darrow's expression grew darker. 'If I were to spend my time chasing Dan Croucher, who is currently outside my area of jurisdiction, I would not be able to fulfil my duties here in Govan. Duties which include running this currently inadequate jail.'

Robinson snorted. 'You raised the subject at the last council meeting. I don't see that there is anything much wrong with the current arrangement.'

Darrow smiled humourlessly. 'Why, I guess that would be because I run the law successfully in spite of the difficulties.'

Hugh ducked his head to hide a smile of his own.

'If so, then why do you wish for change?' Robinson shot back. 'Is the work getting too much for you?'

Hugh emitted a strangled snort. Fortunately for him, the sheriff and the lawyer were too engrossed with one another to notice his reaction to their barbed debate.

Darrow rallied well. 'You forget that I

have effectively been doing the work of two men for the last eight years. My position is sheriff of Govan County, but I have also been acting as marshal of the town of Govan itself. Your concern, Councillor Robinson, is primarily with the town, but I have to consider the needs of the county as well.' He gestured with his right hand. 'Do you really believe this building to be adequate for the needs of a thriving county?'

'How many arrests do you usually make on a weeknight?'

'Weeknights, we might bring four or five in,' Darrow said. 'Fridays and Saturdays can be anything up to fifteen men through each night.'

'There's always more when it's payday on the ranches,' Hugh added.

Darrow nodded. 'There's just not enough room to keep them all in overnight,' he said. 'That's why I'm always asking for less serious cases to be allowed easy bail, so they can go home and free up space for the next night's drunks and brawlers.'

'And those stone cells out the back are perishing cold in winter,' Hugh said. 'I know we only use them for the most violent criminals, but it's not good practice to execute your criminals by letting them freeze to death in their cells.' He shuddered.

'May I see your report book?' Robinson asked.

Darrow gestured for him to sit at the desk. Robinson skimmed through a few pages, slowing down to read one of Hugh's more gossipy reports with a look of distaste.

'You can see the numbers we're bringing in,' Darrow said. 'Govan's the county town. It needs a proper, stone-built gaol.'

'Not on this spot,' Robinson said firmly.

'I thought to the west of the town, south of the river,' Darrow said. 'It'll be easier to separate town law and county law, so I'll move to a new office in town. The town marshal can be based here. Knock down the stone cells at the back and expand the building with a couple more cells like those back there. That'll be enough to hold the drunks and petty criminals that will only be here a day or two before being fined or bailed.'

Robinson glared across the desk at him. 'A town marshal on top of the cost of this new, stone-built gaol and your own salary?' He shook his head.

Darrow leaned over the desk. 'My pay comes from the county, not the town. Govan's not been paying for the law work I've done here the last eight years.'

Hugh moved to join him, facing the lawyer. 'We're taxpayers in this town, but the town's not paying for any law enforcement. And besides, three, or even four of us, can't handle the work of the county and the town any more. Govan's more than doubled in size since I came here.'

Darrow straightened up and smiled humourlessly. 'Like Hugh said, for sure

Govan's getting to be a big town now. Why, we got us a civic hall and a high school now. There's talk of buying a fire engine and raising up a voluntary crew for it. Folks have got a lot more to lose, I reckon.' He paused there, to let Robinson think.

'I bet the *Govan Herald* would feature stories about a new jail,' Hugh added shrewdly. 'Headlines about how the council take law and order seriously.'

'The successful expansion of the town has created a need for expansion of public services,' Darrow carried on. 'Govan continues to grow and thrive.'

Robinson sat back, no doubt considering the favourable headlines in the town's newspaper, and potential votes in the future.

'If the gaol serves the county, it will be built and maintained at the county's expense,' he mused.

'And provide jobs for the town,' Darrow drawled.

Robinson thought for a few moments,

then closed the logbook with a decisive thud. 'Your proposals will be discussed at the next council meeting. I'm still not satisfied with the business of a new marshal and deputies, and of the need to alter this building.'

Darrow's face darkened but he said nothing.

Robinson made his way to the door and paused. 'Have you heard any more from the two criminals you turned loose to rob stagecoaches?'

'I received a telegram last week,' Darrow said stiffly. 'We are working on a plan.'

Robinson snorted. 'Good luck with that, Sheriff. The sooner you give up this nonsense and give your mind to your proper work, the better.'

He left, untroubled by Darrow's vicious glare.

When the door closed, Darrow spat out a curse. Hugh went behind the desk, retrieving his bottle, his glass, and another glass. He poured a shot into the empty glass and silently handed it to

Darrow. The sheriff swallowed half in one go.

'I thought we had him then,' Hugh said. 'He liked the idea of headlines in the newspaper.'

Darrow threw him a glance. 'That was a smart idea to mention it.'

Hugh's eyes widened. 'You just said I had a smart idea!'

'Better make the most of it before it dies of loneliness,' Darrow retorted.

Hugh scowled at him. 'So what is our plan for catching Croucher?'

Darrow paced in front of the desk. 'The intention was for Tomcat and Irish to report back to us on Croucher's whereabouts. However, I think I was correct when I told Robinson that Croucher does not yet trust them. I suspect that he gives them very little information in advance about his plans.' His fist was clenched with frustration.

'So we can't follow him to his destination,' Hugh said. 'If we can't follow, we'll have to lead.'

Darrow stopped short and turned to

look at him, his eyes widening. 'Yes, we'll bait a trap and lead him into it.'

'As Irish suggested in that telegram,' Hugh reminded him.

Darrow nodded curtly. 'Indeed.'

Hugh grinned. 'Set a thief to catch a thief; that's what I first told you, remember?'

'Yes, and *when* we catch Croucher, I'll make sure to thank you nicely.'

Hugh started to smile, but it shrivelled as he took in Darrow's expression.

'So, what kind of bait will you use for the trap?' he asked.

Darrow looked at him coolly. 'I'll do as Irish suggested; I'll go on a well-publicized tax collecting trip that takes me close to the border with Wyoming.'

'When do we go?'

Darrow swallowed the rest of the whiskey. 'I need to allow time for Croucher to get word of my trip. I can't give him as long as I'd like though. I want to do this before the next council meeting. I can't afford to miss that meeting, and if I can bring in Tom Croucher, Robinson will have to agree to my proposals.'

'Arresting Croucher will do wonders for your reputation,' Hugh agreed. 'I didn't mean you have a bad one,' he added hastily. 'Well, not as a sheriff anyway; I just meant that it would be a brave thing to do, and that would make you popular. Not that you aren't anyway; people do ... er ... they admire you.'

Darrow simply stared witheringly at him, then sighed.

⋆　⋆　⋆

Croucher reined in his bay mare and turned to Tomcat Billy. 'I reckon we crossed the border some four-five miles back; for sure we're in Wyoming now.' His smile was cold as the bright blue eyes glanced at Tomcat and Irish. 'You worried yet about being recognized and caught?'

Tomcat nudged his horse past Jackson's and a little closer to the leader. 'I ain't scared,' he replied. 'Shouldn't you be worried 'bout getting caught?'

Croucher stared back, then laughed abruptly. 'I guess so. That being so, you can go on into Holt first, and see if you can get a handle on whereabouts Sheriff Darrow might be.'

Tomcat's grin widened. 'I'm sure enough happy to do that, boss.' He looked back at Irish.

Croucher shook his head. 'I want you alert, not taking it easy with your pal. Gemmill's going with you. Any objection?' he challenged.

'Nope.' Tomcat liked the big, quiet Texan. From the corner of his eye, he could see Fenner moving restlessly, no doubt wanting to object to some part of Croucher's plan.

'Good.' Croucher spoke up as he glanced around at his men, not giving Fenner a chance to speak. Fenner merely glared sullenly at Tomcat. 'Gemmill knows where the rest of us'll be waiting. If you happen to run into the sheriff in town, just you remember that I made a promise to my brother. I aim to be the one that puts Darrow in his grave. If you shoot him, you make damn sure that Gemmill's watching, and can tell me it was pure self-defence an' you didn't provoke him. Understand?'

Tomcat nodded. 'I get it.'

As Gemmill began to turn his horse away from the others, Tomcat turned to Irish and lifted a hand in salute to his friend, before following the big outlaw away.

★ ★ ★

'Have you been here before?' Gemmill asked.

Tomcat looked about at the little town as they rode on to the main street. Most of the buildings were sprawled along this central street. There were stores with painted signs and false fronts, and a couple of saloons, one a genuine two-storey. The fanciest front belonged to the bank. They were passing a telegraph office, and a livery barn on the other side of the street. Further away, he could see the bell tower of a white-painted church, just visible over the shingled roofs around him. A few cottonwoods clustered around the stores and houses, rustling in the prairie wind.

'Not to this place in particular,' Tomcat replied. 'But I sure been to a lot just like it.'

Gemmill grunted, knowing what he meant. 'This place is right at the edge of Darrow's jurisdiction. I'll lay he don't come here more than once in a month of Sundays. Any ideas how we can find him?'

Tomcat pointed to the telegraph and post office. 'Lawmen send notice iffen they're coming on regular visits, things like collecting taxes. Let's see if Darrow's been plumb helpful, telling us where he's gonna be.'

Only a few of the buildings in town

had boardwalks out front. The tele-graph office wasn't one of them, so Tomcat was able to ride his dun up to the noticeboard out front of the small building. He leaned sideways in his saddle to scan the notices that fluttered in the ceaseless prairie breeze. When he picked up the reins again and rode back to Gemmill, there was a bright smile on his face.

'Looks like we sure done picked the right time to come visiting,' he said cheerfully. 'Darrow's coming to these parts real soon. The notice said the twenty-seventh: I don't know for sure what today's date is.'

'Twenty-second, I figure,' Gemmill replied. 'We can ask someplace.'

Tomcat gestured across the street towards the barber shop. 'I got me a hankering for a proper shave an' I kin ask whiles I'm getting one. 'Sides which, it'll look kinda odd iffen we just ride into town, look at a law notice, an' ride straight back out again.'

Gemmill nodded. 'Rusty here's got a

risen clench.' He patted his roan horse on the neck. 'I'll take him to the smith's while you get yourself gussied up, and meet you in the Golden Girl after.'

Tomcat glanced at the larger of the two saloons and smiled. 'Sure thing.'

With amiable nods, they parted to their separate destinations.

11

Croucher had banked most of the gold ingots from the stagecoach robbery while they were in Hot Springs, and had got enough cash out to share liberally among his men, besides letting each one have two ingots apiece. With coins in his pocket, and even notes in his billfold, Tomcat didn't need to account for every cent, as usual. It gave him a sense of freedom. For a few moments, he internally debated the issue of having plentiful, easy money against his dislike of Croucher's murderous ways and his deep-rooted fear of being caught and locked up again. As the barber draped a clean cloth around him, Tomcat decided to forget about it right now and just to enjoy the present.

'Shave and a trim, please,' he drawled, and settled back into the chair to relax and enjoy himself.

By the time the barber was done, it was late morning as Tomcat entered the Golden Girl saloon. A few people had come in for lunch, but as it was a weekday, the place was mostly empty. It just took a quick glance to see that Gemmill hadn't arrived here yet. Tomcat considered spending a little of his wealth on some whiskey, but settled for a beer instead, taking it to a table near the centre of the room. As he sipped the beer, he looked about at the pictures on the walls, which were mostly of women not wearing very much. Appealing though the pictures were, Tomcat's attention was soon diverted by the three live women who entered from a door at the rear. They wore low-cut, gaudily coloured dresses, with skirts that finished at knee height to reveal shapely calves in black stockings. Tomcat's green eyes gleamed as he watched the saloon girls spread out and weave their way between the tables, smiling at the customers.

The one coming closest to him was a short, plump-ish girl, with dark hair cascading down over a red and yellow dress. She smiled at Tomcat as she approached, an endearing dimple appearing in one soft cheek.

'Good morning,' Tomcat drawled, looking at her with frank admiration.

'And to you,' she replied, her southern accent softer than his own.

Tomcat reached out and snagged her wrist, expertly twirling her so she landed in his lap. She gave a gasp of surprise, her full breasts jiggling with the sudden movement. Tomcat slipped his other arm around her waist and smiled.

'My name's Tomcat Billy,' he said.

'Ellie-Mae,' she responded.

He raised an eyebrow and squeezed her with the arm round her waist. 'May she indeed?'

'Why you!' She sounded indignant but she was smiling. 'Tomcat Billy, you are no gentleman to say such a thing.'

'Well, Ellie-Mae, I'm kinda hoping

that you're not a lady.'

'You'll have to talk to me a whiles afore you find out for sure,' she said. 'Iffen you buy me a glass of wine . . . ' She broke off, looking up suddenly.

Tomcat felt and heard movement right behind him. He instantly released his hold on Ellie-Mae, but with her on his lap, he couldn't immediately get out of his chair. Someone grabbed him from behind and yanked him over backwards. Tomcat, Ellie-Mae and the chair all tumbled to the floor together. Ellie-Mae squealed piercingly and grabbed at Tomcat as they fell, hampering him further.

Some part of Ellie-May jabbed into Tomcat's stomach as they hit the floor, driving his breath from him. He was too winded to enjoy the sensation of her wriggling on top of him as she tried to get clear. Her weight suddenly vanished as someone lifted her and threw her to one side.

'Remember you're *my* girl, Ellie!' bellowed a young man. He wore dark trousers and a plaid shirt with the sleeves rolled up to reveal powerful arms.

Tomcat gasped for air, and rolled to one side, trying to get his feet under himself. The young man spun and let fly a kick. Tomcat twisted the other way and the heavy workboot caught him in the side, rolling him on to his face. He kept rolling, brought his legs up and stamped out with a kick against his attacker's knee. The young man staggered back a couple of steps, but as Tomcat started to rise, someone else delivered a kick between his shoulder-blades. Tomcat's face scraped against the floorboards, but he managed to land with his hands down flat. Pushing up, he tried to scramble under the table and out to free space on the other side.

Hands grabbed his leg and hauled him backwards. Tomcat instinctively grabbed the leg of the table, while lashing out with his free foot. He hit the second man on the thigh, to no great effect. Another kick from the first man hit his shoulder, bringing a hiss of pain. As Tomcat twisted towards him, he glimpsed someone large behind his attacker, then the young man rose as he was picked up bodily. Tomcat flattened himself against the floor as the sturdy young man was thrown clean over him, and into the second man. He yanked his leg free as the two attackers hit the ground together in a cursing tangle.

Tomcat bounced upright, almost colliding with Gemmill. The big man's rough-hewn face was looking at the young men with an air of disapproval.

'Thanks,' Tomcat gasped.

'You all right?'

'Jest bruised some.' Tomcat wiped the back of his hand across a sore spot on his face, and turned to look at the two young men.

They'd picked themselves up. The second one, a narrow-eyed, meanly handsome youth, was glaring at Gemmill. The stockier one, who had attacked first, grabbed Ellie-Mae by the arm.

'Haven't I done told you you're my

girl!' he demanded, and slapped her hard across the face.

Ellie-Mae squealed, her dark hair flying as her head rocked under the blow. Tomcat took two fast paces and punched the youth hard in the kidneys. Gemmill grabbed the second man into a bearhug and held him still.

'Only a yellerbelly hits a woman,' spat Tomcat, fists at the ready.

'Break it up!' The barman shoved between the two of them, a short club in his hand. 'I warned you before, Anderson,' he told the youth.

Anderson glared back, his hands coiled into fists. 'The runt was making up to my girl.'

'She was doing her job,' the barman replied. 'The girls get paid to be friendly to all the customers, and you know it. Now you two get out, and if you make trouble again, you'll be barred.'

Gemmill shook the man he was holding, then gave him a contemptuous shove towards the door. The young man kept going, walking sideways so he could watch what his friend was doing. Anderson glared equally at Tomcat, the barman and Ellie-Mae. The girl flinched under his gaze; her cheek was bright red where he'd hit her. Anderson spat in Tomcat's direction, then stormed out, his friend going with him. Gemmill picked up the overturned chair and set it up again.

'I'm sure sorry about that,' Tomcat said to the barman and Ellie-Mae.

The barman shrugged. 'Sorry 'bout Anderson. He's got hisself a real bee in his bonnet about Ellie-Mae.' He nodded to them and headed back to the bar.

Tomcat turned to the girl, holding his hand out to her. 'Are you all right?'

She nodded and took his hand. 'Thank you. I surely do appreciate you standing up for a saloon girl like me.'

'It don't matter what you do,' Tomcat said. 'A man ain't got no business hittin' a woman. I guess he was jealous, but that surely seems like a strange way to treat someone iffen you care about them.'

Ellie-Mae shook her head. 'He makes out like we're courting, but we're not.' She glanced around the saloon and sighed. 'I guess I'll move on. This ain't much of a town anyhow.'

Tomcat nodded. 'Try Govan. They got good law there; if anyone starts acting like Anderson, I just bet the sheriff would knock him straight.'

'I'll remember that.'

Gemmill moved up closer, nodding politely at the girl. 'We've got what we wanted in town,' he said. 'We'd best be getting back to the others.'

'Sure.' Tomcat smiled at Ellie-Mae and gave her a quick kiss on her unhurt cheek. Digging a dollar coin from his pocket, he pressed it into her hand. 'I never did buy you a glass of wine. Spend it on what you like.'

She smiled back. 'Thank you, Tomcat.'

As they rode away from town, Gemmill looked over at Tomcat.

'I was some surprised when you told the girl that Govan has good law.'

Tomcat's green eyes widened. 'So I

did!' He thought about that for a moment. 'Well, it does so, iffen you're not an owlhoot. I guess it'll be some different after we kill Darrow.'

'I guess so.'

★ ★ ★

Irish pulled back the sheet and inspected the straw tick for bedbugs.

'I don't reckon Croucher trusts us,' Tomcat Billy drawled.

Smoothing the sheet back into place, Irish turned and sat on his bed.

'He's said we're gonna be here 'till Darrow comes,' Tomcat continued, gesturing to mean the town, not just their room in the Golden Girl. 'Then after, we're heading back to Colorado. He won't say anything more about where he intends to set ambush.'

'Maybe he ain't decided yet,' Irish suggested.

Tomcat shrugged his narrow shoulders. 'He's been talking to the others all right. An' then he done told us we're not to leave the saloon on our own.'

'He said at least two people with you in case that Anderson comes after you again.'

'Which means either him or one of his men with us,' Tomcat replied. 'You and me should surely be enough to manage Anderson and his friend iffen they feel like making trouble.' He shook his head. 'Croucher don't trust us out of his sight.'

Irish gave a snort of amusement. 'For sure it's strange: outlaws don't trust us, but Sheriff Darrow does.'

'Case of 'have to', for Darrow,' Tomcat replied, though a brief grin showed his appreciation of the irony.

'We got to find a way of wiring Darrow to let him know where we are,' Irish said, turning to watch as Tomcat headed towards the window and opened it. 'And as soon as possible, so he's got time to fix up whatever he's planning.'

When Croucher had said they were staying in Holt to wait for the sheriff, Tomcat had chosen a room at the back of the saloon. The shingled roof of the one-storey kitchen was below and to one side of their window. Irish wouldn't have been able to get in or out without using a rope, but to Tomcat, it was just a nice little exercise.

He was smiling again as he turned round, his face bright with mischief.

'I figure I can manage that.' His smile widened. 'And have me some fun, too.'

★ ★ ★

The saloon was a little busier in the early evening than it had been at lunch-time. Croucher and his men had gathered at a large table in the centre of the room. Jackson was sitting alone at one end, his nose in a dime novel detective story. Croucher, Fenner, Gemmill and Irish were playing a sporadic poker game for pennies. Tomcat Billy had another deck and was using it to build a house of cards while watching the game. He carefully added another pair of cards before speaking to Croucher.

'You figured out what we're gonna do yet?'

Croucher just nodded, watching Fenner as the young man studied his cards. Fenner snorted in disgust and slapped his cards down on the table, shaking his head.

'You know where we're gonna be waiting for Darrow?' Tomcat persisted.

Croucher nodded again, his face locked in its usual slight frown. He pushed six cents into the middle of the table and looked expectantly at Gemmill. The big man sipped from his glass of water, and added eight cents to the pot. Fenner picked up a cent from his small pile and flicked it across the table into Tomcat's house of cards, scattering them. Tomcat snatched up the coin and drew back his hand, to throw it, but halted himself. Fenner's boyish face smirked across the table at him.

'You was pretty squeamish when I took out that stagecoach guard,' Fenner said. 'How come you're so keen to deal with that sheriff?'

Tomcat pocketed the coin. 'The guard didn't do me no wrong. With Darrow, it's personal.'

'I'm out.' Irish folded his cards and put them on the table.

'Guess I got you all wrong.' Fenner's tone was patronizing. 'I had you all figured for a lily-livered, two-bit owl-hoot, not someone who's man enough to even talk about wanting to kill a sheriff.'

Tomcat's voice was low but hard. 'And I had you figured out as someone smart enough not to yak about who they killed, right in the middle of a saloon.'

Gemmill gave a rumble of laughter. Fenner started to stand up but Croucher gave him a sharp smack across the shoulder.

'Tomcat's right,' he snapped. 'Quit ragging on him and try acting a bit smarter.'

Fenner glared across the table at Tomcat, who was gathering the scattered cards together. Tomcat ignored him, and glanced about the saloon. His face lit up when he saw Ellie-Mae near the bar, and he waved her across.

'How are you?' he asked, as she reached him.

If Anderson's slap had left any mark on her face, it was disguised by makeup. She was wearing a different dress, this one in pink and black, but as revealing as the other.

'I'm fine, thank you,' Ellie-Mae answered. 'I done booked me a ticket on the next stage through to Govan.'

'That's swell.' Tomcat smiled. 'Now, we was doing something afore we got interrupted by Anderson.' He pushed his chair back, snagged her wrist and had her on his lap in one smooth move. Ellie-Mae giggled, her eyes wide with surprise.

'Why, you sure are a wicked man, Tomcat Billy,' she exclaimed.

He pushed her thick dark hair aside and nuzzled the back of her neck. 'I'm wicked,' he admitted. 'But I ain't bad. In fact, I reckon to be pretty good.' He slipped his other hand under her skirt and up her thigh.

Croucher took no notice of Tomcat's actions, other than to direct a warning glance at Fenner. He looked at his cards again, then matched Gemmill's bet. Gemmill took the hand, with three tens to Croucher's pairs of queens and nines. Johnson raised his head, looked around the table as he took a mouthful of beer, then went back to his book. Gemmill took the pot and gathered up the cards, glancing at Irish, who smiled.

'Deal me in,' Irish said, unconcerned by Tomcat's behaviour.

Gemmill shuffled the deck, his large hands engulfing the cards. 'I can see how your friend got called Tomcat.'

Irish glanced over the table at Tomcat and Ellie-Mae, who were getting on famously. 'He sure earned it.' The nickname had originally referred to Tomcat's agility and climbing skills, but Irish thought it wiser not to mention that. There was no point in alerting Croucher to Tomcat's ability to get in and out of buildings without using a door.

By the time Croucher had taken the next hand, Tomcat was whisking a quivering Ellie-Mae away to the privacy of his room. Gemmill watched them head up the stairs in the corner of the room.

'He never even bought her a drink,' he remarked.

Irish shrugged his broad shoulders. 'Like he said, he's pretty good.'

'It don't take much to please a half-dollar floozy like that,' Fenner said scornfully.

Irish turned his mildest face on the young man. 'Whatever it takes, you sure ain't got it; for sure, she never even glanced at you.'

Gemmill rumbled with laughter again. 'You'd better quit, Fenner. It's your tail keeps getting twisted.'

12

Tomcat yawned, stretched leisurely and rolled over on his rumpled bed.

'I sure did enjoy that,' he drawled. 'I'm mighty grateful to you, Ellie-Mae.'

She pulled her stockings and drawers out of the tangle of clothes on the floor, and sat on the edge of Irish's bed, facing towards Tomcat.

'You stood up for me earlier, when Anderson hit me,' she answered, pulling on the drawers. 'I surely did enjoy paying you back.'

'You got to git dressed already?' Tomcat enquired lazily.

Ellie-Mae nodded. 'I'm supposed to be working. I can't quit town until the next stage comes through and that's another three days.'

Tomcat stretched a sinewy arm out of bed to pick up his brown corduroy trousers. Sitting up, he extracted three five-dollar bills from his billfold. 'Give your boss one to make up for the drinks I should have bought you. Keep the others for a grubstake.'

Ellie-Mae hesitated, then took the cash. 'Thank you.' Her eyes were more eloquent.

'That's all right.' Tomcat lay down and yawned again. 'You plumb tuckered me out; I'm feeling as slow as molasses in wintertime. I'd be mighty grateful iffen you'd tell my friends I'm gonna take a nap. I'll be back down in about an hour or so.'

'Sure,' Ellie-Mae nodded.

Tomcat relaxed and enjoyed watching her get dressed again. When she was ready, she bent over to give him a quick kiss on the cheek, and Tomcat got in a quick pat on her plump bottom. Ellie-Mae giggled as she left. Tomcat lay still and listened, hearing the thump of her high-heeled boots fade away along the corridor. As soon as she was out of earshot, he slipped out of the bed and began rapidly donning his clothes.

A couple of minutes later he was at the window, which he'd left open. After a quick glance about, Tomcat Billy climbed through and made the awkward jump on to the roof of the kitchen, landing lightly on his moccasinned feet. He moved quickly and quietly to the far end and climbed down in moments, strong fingers and toes finding purchase on the narrow frame of the door. Sparing time for a quick glance up at the window he'd started from, Tomcat grinned with pride, and set off briskly around the back of the neighbouring store.

★ ★ ★

Irish looked up from the game as Tomcat's saloon girl sauntered across to their table. There was a smile at the corners of her mouth and a distinct air of self-satisfaction about her. Fenner muttered something under his breath, and made a show of studying his cards as the girl stopped by Irish's chair.

'Are you doing all right?' Irish asked her, glancing past her in search of Tomcat.

She smiled. 'Why sure. Tomcat was fixing to sleep a whiles. He done asked me to tell you he'd be down in near about an hour.'

Irish smiled widely in return, to cover his immediate feeling of surprise. He'd never known Tomcat take a nap after one of his saloon girl flings before. The story about the nap had to be an excuse for something, and in moments, Irish guessed what it probably was. The girl gave him a saucy wink and strolled off.

'I never knew anyone needed to sleep after tumbling a little whore like that,' Fenner remarked scornfully.

Irish raised an eyebrow. 'Why surely you've heard of a cat nap?'

Gemmill laughed and even Croucher's long face loosened into a smile.

Johnson looked up briefly from his book, then went back to the lurid tale.

'Still, Tomcat needed more than a cat nap after he got himself tangled up with this woman in Nebraska,' Irish said, glancing around at the others. 'She was a sweet bit with plenty of stamina, but the real trouble was when her husband found out what had been going on. Tomcat didn't hardly stop running all night.'

He continued on with the stories as the card game slowly continued. If Tomcat was doing what Irish suspected, it was important that Croucher and his men remain in the saloon until Tomcat showed up again.

* * *

The telegraph office was just across the dusty street, but Tomcat Billy lingered against the side wall of a general store. When he'd slipped out of the bedroom, a couple of minutes before, he'd had every intention of telegraphing Sheriff Darrow to let the lawman know that Croucher was waiting for him in Holt. Faced with the reality, he found himself hesitating. That telegram would commit him to aiding the lawman whose testimony had got him locked into that soul destroying gaol.

It was also an act of betrayal to Croucher and his men. Tomcat had no fondness for Croucher's willingness to shoot and downright despised Fenner's eagerness to kill. He had to admit that Darrow would be doing the world a favour by getting rid of those two. Johnson, he had no strong feelings about, and Gemmill, Tomcat rather liked. Gemmill's easy-going nature and size reminded him of Irish. The thought of his old friend made Tomcat shift restlessly.

He still found it hard to believe that Irish would leave him in order to go straight. If he thought a little, he could imagine Irish as an honest worker of some sort. It was much harder to think of Irish walking away from him, and Tomcat realized that the difficulty was because he didn't want to see his friend turn his back. In the five or so years they'd been pals, they'd shared everything, with barely a cross word. Not once, since leaving home in Tennessee, had Tomcat met anyone he trusted the way he trusted Irish. That last thought reminded him of something that Irish had said earlier, about trust.

A brawny, unshaven man glanced curiously at him, as he ambled past in the direction of the saloon. Most likely he was just looking at a stranger in the small town, as anyone would. It still gave Tomcat a jolt. He didn't know if the man was heading for the saloon, and even if he was, it was unlikely he would mention Tomcat Billy's presence between the buildings to anyone. All the same, Tomcat couldn't risk word getting back to Croucher.

What he did know was that Croucher didn't trust him, but that Darrow was trusting him to do a job. Tomcat's sense of fair play told him that, really, Darrow had only been doing his own job in sending Tomcat to prison. Being punished for doing something wrong seemed perfectly fair to him, and he'd known perfectly well that theft was wrong. Tomcat suddenly realized that although he'd blamed Darrow for the misery he'd suffered in prison, Darrow hadn't been malicious. Arresting criminals was simply what the sheriff did, just like some men sold shirts, and some herded cattle. Ordinary people, like his folk back home, needed men like Sheriff Darrow far more than they needed men like Croucher and Fenner.

The thoughts passed through Tomcat's mind in a flash. They were more like feelings than a coherent argument, but the result was strong enough to send him trotting over the street and into the telegraph office.

★　★　★

Some twenty minutes later he came strolling down the stairs into the main room of the Golden Girl saloon. Getting a beer first, he joined the lively group at the table, seating himself beside his friend.

'Are you all right, an' all?' Irish

183

asked, shuffling the cards.

Tomcat smiled and nodded. 'Why sure I am. Everything's plumb good. You kin deal me in.'

Irish smiled back. 'For sure.'

★   ★   ★

'Telegram come for you.' Baldwin held the brown envelope over the desk.

Darrow almost snatched it from his hand and tore it open. His dark eyes flickered over the few words on the thin paper.

In holt with the captain stop the boys are planning a surprise party for your visit stop don't have details but expect it outside town stop tomcat

Darrow stayed still for a long moment, then looked up. 'Go find Pacey and Hugh.'

'Hugh's at home with Mrs Keating and the baby,' Baldwin reminded him. 'He's off duty.'

Darrow simply continued to stare at him until the deputy nodded and left briskly.

★　★　★

Twenty minutes later, all four lawmen were assembled in the law office. Darrow was in his chair behind the leather-topped desk. Hugh, jacketless and with his shirt sleeves rolled up, was in the other chair. He was taking intermittent bites from a beef sandwich hastily assembled from his interrupted dinner. Pacey was by the weapons rack on the rear wall, rubbing an oiled cloth over the barrels of a shotgun. Baldwin was a little further away; he rested his weight on the narrow sill of the front window.

The new deputy was a striking-looking young man. Seth Baldwin was just above average height, broad shoul-dered and ruggedly attractive, with wide cheekbones and a strong chin. His curly hair, cropped short, was dark brown with a rusty tinge. Skin the colour of milky coffee told of mixed parentage, a generation or two back. His eyes were unexpectedly light in colour, being the green-tinted brown of hazel. He watched and listened, fascinated, as the others talked.

'You think Tomcat's telling the truth?' Pacey asked the sheriff.

'He has to be.' Darrow's expression was intense.

'If he was lying, he'd have made up more details,' Hugh said, tilting his head back to look up at Pacey. 'He'd specify a place and time to make sure we were where he, or Croucher, wanted us to be.'

'Unless he's trying to double-bluff us,' Pacey suggested. 'You know, making us think Croucher doesn't really trust him and won't tell him anything in advance, so we trust him more and go haring off to Holt on his say-so.'

'Too risky,' Hugh said confidently. 'No matter how many layers of bluff you suspect, without details, there's no guarantee they'd be in the right place at the right time.' He took a bite of sandwich and licked a smudge of mustard off his thumb.

'I hate to say it, but I think Hugh's right,' Darrow drawled. 'Croucher and his men will surely be planning to ambush me when I ride to Holt on this tax collecting trip, but we can't be sure where they'll be.' He paused for a moment, thinking. 'I'm due there on the twenty-seventh; today's the twenty-second. We've just got nice time to do it!' He lifted his head, his eyes flashing. His whole body was bristling with energy, keen to be moving. 'We'll get down there on the twenty-sixth, check the ground for likely ambush spots, and then set up in wait for them.'

Pacey rattled the shotgun back on to the rack. 'I like it. Who's going?'

Darrow glanced round at the others. 'You, me and Baldwin, for certain. I'd like to have a couple more men along if possible. Hugh, you can stay here and mind the office.'

Hugh sat upright on his chair, putting his plate on the desk. 'I'm coming with you,' he said, looking hurt.

'Since when did you start volunteering to be a hero?' Darrow drawled.

Hugh's mild face took on a stubborn look. 'I took on that responsibility when you swore me in as a deputy.'

Darrow's expression softened slightly, compassion in his eyes. 'Things have changed since then, Hugh. You've got Minnie and Rose depending on you now.'

'I revised my will when Rose was born,' Hugh said with dignity. 'The house is paid for outright, and there's enough money invested to keep them both comfortably for their lifetimes.'

'Rose can't buy herself another father.'

Hugh flinched slightly but didn't drop his gaze. 'I know that. But if I am going to be a deputy, I'm going to do the job properly, at least for the important things,' he added honestly. 'Minnie's proud of me for being an officer of the law, and I want Rose to be proud of me as well.

Letting my friends shoulder all the dangerous work while I stay behind isn't something to be proud of.'

'Dead, and honourable, is still dead,' Darrow drawled.

'If you've got the right to risk your life, I've got the right to risk mine,' Hugh insisted. 'I'm coming with you.'

'Why?'

'Because you need one person there that you trust absolutely.'

It was Darrow who dropped his gaze first. He acknowledged Hugh's statement with a slight nod and a grateful look, then turned to Baldwin, all fierce business again.

'Baldwin, you'll stay here and mind the office.'

'Yes, sir.' Baldwin's voice was deep and musical. He studied Hugh thoughtfully, noting the deep breaths the Englishman took, as if to calm his nerves.

'We'll leave noon on the twenty-fourth,' Darrow announced. 'That's the day after tomorrow. Be prepared for a long ride; get your horse's shoes checked. We'll overnight in Ridgeville on the way down.' He sighed. 'We have to get Croucher first time. I've got to be back here for a council meeting on the thirtieth.'

'We should take a spare mount or two,' Pacey suggested.

Darrow nodded. 'I'll arrange something with Norman.' He stood up and looked across at Baldwin. 'Take over Pacey's patrol this evening.'

'Sure thing, boss.' Baldwin unhitched himself from the windowsill and went to pick up a shotgun.

Darrow took his black hat down from the coat pegs and set it on. 'I'm going to speak to Whiskers. If he can get someone to cover for him at the telegraph office, I'd like to have him with us.'

'Whiskers is a dab hand at reading tracks,' Hugh explained to Baldwin. 'Do you think Josh would come along?' he suggested to the sheriff.

'We could use another gun,' Pacey said. 'We're going to be outnumbered.'

Hugh blinked as he did a quick mental calculation. 'Don't forget Tomcat and

Irish are really with us. If Whiskers comes, we'll be six against Croucher's four.'

'That's *if* Tomcat and Irish are really on our side, and willing to fight with us,' Pacey replied.

'If they're not, then we shoot them too,' Darrow said, ending the conversation as he left the office.

13

'Be good for Mama while Daddy's away.' Hugh stroked his daughter's peach-soft cheek and was rewarded with a sudden, gummy grin.

'Oh! That was her first smile!' Minnie hitched up the tightly wrapped bundle in her arms and gazed lovingly into her baby's face.

Beyond Hugh, the wide front door of their home was already open, letting in the warmth of the early summer's day. Hugh's horse, with bed-roll and kit fastened behind the saddle, dozed patiently by the gate.

'Really?' Hugh leaned close and repeated his action a couple of times, being rewarded with another grin and soft cooing noises from Rose. In spite of the evidence in front of him, it was rather hard to believe that he was actually a father. After the first shock of her actual arrival, he was becoming fascinated with his baby and all the little changes as she developed and became more responsive. Straightening up again, he took a reluctant step away.

'I really have to go,' he said regretfully.

Minnie dug something out of her skirt pocket and handed it to him.

'I got this for you.' It was a gold fob locket, with Saint Christopher depicted on the cover. Hugh carefully prised it open: inside was a dark blonde lock of Minnie's hair, overlaid with a few pale blonde wisps of Rose's short fuzz. He looked at it for a few moments, then closed the locket again and smiled at his wife.

'I don't need anything to remind me of you both, but it's nice to feel that we won't be entirely separated.' Hugh attached the locket to his watch chain. 'Thank you,' he said sincerely, and kissed Minnie warmly.

'I know you'll take care of yourself,' she said afterwards. 'I'm glad you're going, because Beau needs you.' She was the only person in Govan who ever thought of Sheriff Beauchief Darrow by his first name. 'He'd never admit it,' she added. 'But this business with Croucher has shaken him, and he needs a friend.'

Hugh smiled. 'I think you're right, but I'll spare his feelings and not tell him so.'

With a last peck on Rose's cheek, he took a deep breath and walked out of the door.

★　★　★

By the following afternoon, Darrow and his men were in the welcome shade of a mixed stand of pine, aspen and shrubs, some ten miles north of Holt. The main trail was on open ground, but they'd left it and stopped in cover on the rising ground just to the east that was the foothills of the Sierra Madres. Darrow dismounted first, loosening his horse's girths and giving Gabriel a quick pat on the neck before he turned to face the others. All had dismounted too, and were giving their horses a quick check. Hugh's mare had an itchy spot on her face, and rubbed her head vigorously against him, almost knocking him off his feet. Pacey was methodically checking his horse's hoofs. Whiskers, the wiry old former prospector, stood quietly, his disreputable hat pulled down over his eyes. Darrow's gaze lingered longest on the unknown element in his party. Josh Turnage had been unable to come due to work commitments. Instead, Darrow had agreed to hire Ben Donnington, a cowhand who had drifted into town a few days earlier, looking for work. He'd struck up an acquaintance with Whiskers in the Empty Lode saloon, and Darrow had grudgingly taken the old-timer's recommendation.

Finished with his horse, Pacey straightened up, and strode over to face Darrow.

'So what's the plan?' He stood braced, as though on parade.

Darrow's pose was deliberately casual. 'Were you not listening when I told you all back in Govan, or have you forgotten since?' he drawled.

Pacey looked scornful. 'Neither. But your brilliant plan was no more detailed than getting here first and setting up in ambush for Croucher and his men. We're in the right part of Wyoming, but we need to scout the country and plan our campaign.'

Darrow stared back at him for a moment, then unexpectedly smiled. 'Well now, if we're planning a military campaign, maybe we should use the expertise of a former army officer we happen to have amongst us.' He nodded at Pacey. 'You must be the most qualified man for the job, Lieutenant Pacey.'

Hugh opened his mouth to speak, aware that Darrow had served as a captain during the Civil War, then closed it again and watched thoughtfully.

Pacey nodded, looking pleased. 'I'll take Whiskers, and we'll scout the land ahead and find somewhere to lie in wait for Croucher.'

Darrow agreed, and watched as

Pacey and Whiskers remounted and rode away. When they were out of sight, Hugh strolled over to the sheriff.

'That was very clever,' he remarked.

Darrow gave him a bland look.

'If Pacey picks a good spot, we should catch or kill Croucher,' Hugh said. 'If he picks a bad spot and Croucher gets away, then you get to blame Pacey for it. Either way, you can't lose.'

'Croucher getting away is not winning, though,' Darrow said darkly. 'And I'm a bad loser.'

*　　*　　*

Irish found himself yawning, and belatedly covered his mouth with his hand. He caught a sympathetic look from Gemmill, riding on his right, and acknowledged it with a smile. Croucher had insisted on them all rising very early in order to ride out ready for Sheriff Darrow's expected arrival later that day. Darrow wasn't likely to arrive in Holt before mid-morning but the outlaw wasn't taking any chances: he wanted his men ready and waiting in good time.

Fenner had been sent ahead to scout, and now came back, his horse moving at a fast lope. He reached the rest of the outlaws and reined his bay mare in hard, halting in a flurry of dirt. Croucher gave him a cold look as the horse shook her head and fretted against the tight reins.

'You'll spoil her legs, pulling her up like that,' he admonished.

Fenner's face split in a grin. 'Why, Mandy's legs are as hard as steel,' he bragged.

'Steel ain't indestructible. You need a sound horse to outrun trouble an' it's plumb foolish to spoil a good one by riding like a drunk greenhorn,' Croucher snapped. He was silent a moment, his blue eyes cold, before speaking more calmly. 'Did you see anything?'

Fenner's boyish face was sullen but he answered mildly. 'There ain't nothing moving; it's as quiet as the grave out there.'

Croucher nodded once. 'Good.' He made a curt gesture towards the ground just ahead. 'We'll get up on that ridge and take cover in those trees.'

Irish studied the area indicated, trying to keep his expression bland, though his stomach was uneasy with nerves. The ground on the right side of the trail rose to a low ridge that was the lowest foothill of the edge of the range to the east. It was fairly densely wooded, in contrast to the flatter, more open ground to the west. It was divided about a third of the way along by a wide draw that led up towards the higher ground behind. Croucher was giving out his orders.

'The horses will be hidden in that draw. Give them a little grain and make sure they're comfortable. Gemmill, I want you and Tomcat on the far side of the draw, 'bout where them choke cherries are. Jackson, you and Irish are on the near side, about level with them. Me an' Fenner will be beyond the draw, near to that birch.' He pointed to a clump of trees with distinctive white, papery bark, visible among the darker conifers.

As Croucher talked, Irish looked across at Tomcat, who was on his left. Tomcat's green eyes were scanning the forested area ahead but Irish couldn't tell if he was looking for good hiding places, or hoping that Darrow was already there. His friend had said that he'd wired a warning to the sheriff, but for the first time in years, Irish didn't have complete and utter trust in Tomcat. He wanted to; he wanted his friend to be willing to help Darrow, and quit the lawless life, but a small part of him feared that Tomcat was more interested in revenge on the man who'd put him in prison. Occupied with his worries, and half-listening to Croucher, Irish didn't notice his horse pricking its ears and lifting its head to sniff the light breeze.

The bay gelding suddenly let out a prolonged neigh, its sides shuddering with the effort. Irish snapped to full alertness, aware that the horse was gazing at the trees ahead. The other men also lost their relaxed pose, straightening up and turning heads. Moments later, another, unseen, horse replied, the whinny coming from among the trees in the draw. Croucher grabbed for his rifle. Fenner had a pistol half drawn when a shot kicked up dirt in front of his horse. The bay shied, making him lurch in the saddle, and turned away from the trees. The other horses snorted and sidled away, partially distracting their riders' attention as they regained control.

'Drop your weapons now!'

It was Darrow's voice; the sheriff was somewhere among the trees, where Croucher had intended to set up ambush. If the riders had travelled another fifty yards before halting, they would have been almost under the sheriff's gun. As it was, Croucher had stopped just before drawing level with the edge of the tree cover. If the sheriff had spread his men out in the way

Croucher had intended, most of them would be at a long rifle shot from where the outlaws stood.

Croucher's blue eyes blazed with fury but he didn't waste time in speech.

'Run!'

As he spoke, he reined his horse around and spurred the mare into a dead run.

There was no time for debate, no time to think. As horses burst into action and gunfire opened up, Irish just acted. Slamming his heels into his horse's sides, he forced it to gallop away from the others, towards the trees. He had to trust the lawmen wouldn't mistake his actions and shoot him. Most of all, he had to hope that Tomcat would do the same, and ride away from the outlaws and life on the run.

Hugh fired after the fleeing outlaws but they were quickly out of range, with no apparent damage done. He started to work the action of his rifle again, but Darrow, crouched a couple of feet away, caught his arm.

'We go after them, now!' the sheriff barked. He rose fast, hauling Hugh to his feet, and shoved his deputy towards the draw.

Hugh stumbled through the trees, clumsy on the sloping ground. Darrow passed him, concentrating on covering the ground as fast as possible. The ground dropped away as they reached the edge of the draw. Hugh skidded on loose soil, barely keeping his balance as he stumbled down the slope. Only a wild grab at a pine branch kept him from reaching the bottom flat on his face. Breathless and off-balance, he saw Pacey and Donnington tightening cinches and getting the horses ready.

Donnington took Gabriel's reins and led the black across to Darrow as the sheriff approached. Darrow didn't thank him, just grabbed the reins and threw himself into the saddle. The cowhand stared after the sheriff as Darrow spun his horse and sent it racing down the draw.

'What about Whiskers?' he asked

Hugh, who was heading for his own horse.

The old-timer had been waiting on the far side of the draw and wasn't visible yet.

'He'll follow on,' Hugh answered, shoving his rifle into its boot. 'Get moving.'

A minute later, Hugh had ridden clear of the draw and on to the trail. Darrow was only a little way down the trail, talking to Tomcat Billy and Irish. Hugh had seen them ride away from the other outlaws but had been too busy concentrating on Croucher to watch what they had been doing.

'Where's Croucher headed to?' the sheriff demanded. His pistol was in his hand and not quite aimed at the two freed outlaws.

'For sure he'll be after going back to Colorado,' Irish rumbled.

'Whereabouts? Steamboat Springs?'

'He wouldn't tell us outright.' Tomcat's face had an unusually hard expression. 'He didn't trust us none. And 'sides, even iffen he done tole us, he wouldn't go there iffen he reckons as we might tell you.'

Darrow's face darkened: Hugh guessed it was with anger at himself. Normally Darrow would have thought of that last point himself but his bitterness towards Croucher was affecting his usual clear-headed thinking. The sheriff was normally a tightly self-controlled man but cracks were beginning to show in that façade and it worried Hugh. Without another word, Darrow kicked his horse into a gallop and set off after the outlaws.

Tomcat turned to Hugh as he rode up.

'We kept our word,' he said immediately. 'We gave you a shot at Croucher.'

Hugh nodded. 'You did. I'll see you get treated right.' He twisted in his saddle to see Pacey and Donnington emerging from the draw at a fair pace. Turning back, he glanced ahead to Darrow, who was pushing his horse hard, and not looking back. 'You've done what we asked,' he said to Tomcat and Irish. 'But I'd be grateful if you'd ride along and help us out now.'

The two friends looked at one another.

'If we're goin' straight, it can't hurt to have lawmen as pals,' Tomcat drawled.

Irish's face split with a wide smile. 'For sure, you're right.'

'Then let's ride.' Hugh dug his heels into his horse's sides and set off.

The outlaws had a short head start, but their horses had already travelled some four miles that morning. It wasn't a great distance, but the lawmen's mounts were fresher. Hugh and the others were soon travelling in a loose group, some quarter of a mile behind the sheriff. Darrow was pushing his horse hard, and Gabriel responded with the courage of his fine breeding. The morning was becoming hot and Gabriel's sweat whipped into white foam around his girth, but he kept going gallantly.

The country here was fairly open, but

Darrow was lost to view now and again as the ground undulated. Hugh kept going fast enough to keep in touch, but didn't want to risk having his horse break down. Nor did he want to leave Tomcat and Irish behind, as their horses had already covered the distance out from town that morning. Pacey pushed his showy chestnut on a little faster and drew ahead as the chase continued.

First the outlaws, and then Darrow, disappeared from sight as they followed the trail down into a dip in the prairie. Hugh didn't know this country well, but he had an overall idea of the land.

He shouted across to Tomcat. 'Isn't that a long slope head? Down to a stream?'

'There's a creek, sure,' Tomcat answered.

Hugh was slightly breathless from the long gallop, but he shook the reins and urged his mare on faster as Pacey approached the top of the slope. When he reached it, he had a wide view over the valley below. Pacey was keeping his horse to a controlled lope downhill but Darrow had barely slowed from his hard gallop. Not too far ahead of him now, the outlaws were splashing through the shallow creek that crossed the trail. Hugh reined in his mare a little as she began to increase speed down the slope.

As the outlaws reached the far bank of the creek, they halted and turned their horses. Hugh was grabbing for his rifle even before the outlaws began to reach for theirs. He forgot to worry about galloping downhill, with only one hand on the reins and a heavy rifle unbalancing him. All that concerned him was Darrow, riding headlong towards a bunch of outlaws who were drawing their guns on him. Pacey, further down-slope from Hugh, was halting his horse as he drew his rifle, but Hugh kept going, still too far away for even a half-decent shot. He saw Darrow belatedly reach for his pistol, then the outlaws fired in ragged sequence.

It seemed to happen very fast.

Gabriel took another stride, then his legs buckled and the black crashed to the ground and rolled over. Darrow was thrown clear, hitting hard before also rolling and sliding over the dusty ground. Pacey fired back immediately, pouring bullets at the outlaws as fast as he could work the action of his Winchester. Hugh looped his reins once round the saddlehorn and threw his rifle to his shoulder, letting off quick, wild shots. Around him came the crash of more rifles: Whiskers, Donnington, Irish and Tomcat, all charging down the slope and firing fast. They knew they were unlikely to hit. They just had to distract the outlaws:

14

A swift glance showed Hugh that Darrow was moving, though not much. A glance was all he had time for. His horse was plunging, excited and almost uncontrolled, down a slope. All he could do was try to stay in the bumping saddle while firing his rifle, praying he didn't accidentally hit the fallen sheriff. He felt sick in his stomach, and everything stank of sweat and gunpowder, but Hugh kept going. Croucher was firing towards Darrow, other outlaws fired towards the approaching lawmen. Their horses were moving restlessly, agitated by the sounds and movement.

One of the outlaws, a large man, shouted something to the others. He shoved his rifle back in its boot and took up his reins. Now Hugh could hear him shouting Croucher's name as the outlaw leader tried to get an accurate shot at Darrow, telling Croucher to run. Croucher's horse suddenly threw its head up and shied sideways, grazed or frightened by a bullet. The big outlaw, Gemmill, rode his horse against Croucher's forcing it to turn away. One of the other outlaws had also booted his rifle and was running for it. The shortest one fired a couple more shots up the slope, cursing furiously, then stopped firing to haul his bay around by a fierce pull on the reins. He kicked the horse into a hard gallop, still clutching his rifle in one hand.

A few uneven shots went after the fleeing outlaws. Hugh grabbed his reins and began bringing his horse back to a slower pace. His attention was now all on the sheriff, who was sitting up. As Hugh steered his horse across to him, Darrow stared stiffly at the running outlaws for a few, still moments. Then the sheriff turned abruptly, and crawled a few feet to sit on the ground beside his fallen horse. Hugh slowed his blowing mount to a walk and stopped a few feet away to dismount. Darrow took no notice, his attention fixed on Gabriel.

The black horse had stopped trying to rise. He lay on his side, the barrel of his chest rising and falling irregularly. Bright blood stained the glossy black hide in several places, and ran from the flaring nostrils. Darrow sat silently, his face hidden by the brim of his hat, as one hand repetitively stroked the horse's neck. Hugh approached quietly and knelt down on the other side of the horse. Darrow's shoulders tensed slightly, but he didn't look up.

The others had caught up. They dismounted, seeing to their blowing mounts, speaking quietly. Hugh looked at the dying horse, shuddering at the blood, then looked at the sheriff, trying to see any sign of injury. Darrow's face was oddly bewildered, and hurt, as though he couldn't understand what had happened to his horse. It was a look Hugh had never seen before, and it frightened him.

'He trusted me,' Darrow said slowly. 'I failed him.'

Hugh swallowed, and gently touched

the other man on the shoulder.

'Darrow? We have to ... ' He changed his mind and started to rise, trying to get Darrow to stand too. 'Come on,' he pleaded. 'Let's move away a little.'

'No.' The word was clear. Darrow looked at Hugh, his eyes now sharply focussed. 'It's my responsibility: I have to finish it.' His hand lingered on the horse's neck a few moments longer, then went to his holster.

It was empty; he'd had the pistol in his hand when Gabriel had fallen, and it had been dropped. Hugh hastily drew his Webley and offered it butt first. Darrow took the heavy pistol, pulling back the hammer. He changed position slightly, placing the muzzle of the gun in the centre of the horse's forehead. The sheriff's hand was steady as he pulled the trigger. The black horse shuddered, one hind leg kicking reflexively, then lay still. The laboured breathing stopped. The air smelt sharply of gunpowder, blood and sweat.

Darrow remained still for a moment, then abruptly handed the pistol back to Hugh. He rose and turned to face the others, who had gathered together nearby. Hugh stood too, waiting slightly to one side.

'Thank you.' The words were formal but there was gratitude in the sheriff's eyes. 'All of you, especially you two.' He nodded at Tomcat Billy and Irish. 'Croucher won't get away. It may take months, or years, but sooner or later he will be caught or killed. I aim to have a hand in it somehow. Right now, I need to wire Baldwin, and the state marshals' office, so I'm going on to Holt.' He spoke specifically to Tomcat and Irish again. 'You two are free to go where you want; I'll make sure those pardons are issued in full.'

The two men glanced at one another; it was Tomcat who answered.

'I guess we'll ride with you for now, sheriff.'

Darrow nodded, and went to pick up his gun.

Hugh sipped his whiskey and studied Darrow from across the table in the Golden Girl saloon. The sheriff had a neat pile of telegraph forms, and was busy writing messages to be wired to state marshals and other law enforcement agencies. He paused a moment, aware of being watched, then continued without looking up. However he felt about the events earlier in the morning, he was keeping it to himself.

Looking around, Hugh saw Whiskers, Tomcat, Irish and Donnington at a table by the window, playing euchre. Pacey was sitting at a table by himself, cleaning his guns. The only other people in the room were the barman, who was talking to a squinty-eyed man leaning against the bar, and a solitary saloon girl knitting a red shawl. Hugh's attention wandered back to the card game, where Donnington was discussing scoring rules with Irish and Whiskers. Tomcat, his cards carefully held close to his chest, was gazing out of the window.

Tomcat suddenly tensed, then leaned closer to the glass. Hugh felt a jolt of fear and took a bracing swig of the whiskey.

'There's a rider coming in hell for leather,' Tomcat announced. Heads turned to him as he kept looking out. 'I reckon . . . yes, he done rode out jus' five minutes ago!' He looked over at the lawmen, who were already coming to their feet.

Darrow sprinted to the door of the saloon, followed by his deputies. They could all hear the galloping horse approaching. Darrow flung the door open as a ranch hand hauled his horse to a sliding stop outside.

'Croucher's coming!' the ranch hand yelled. 'He's loaded for bear!'

With that, he dug spurs into his horse and raced along the dirt street, yelling warnings to the few people about. Darrow glanced the way the man had come, then quickly stepped back inside.

'Donnington, Whiskers: upstairs, front rooms.' The orders came fast and decisive. 'Civilians: all of you get upstairs now. Stay out of sight.'

As he finished speaking, Tomcat Billy sprinted past and through the door, Irish pounding along behind him.

'Trust us!' Irish said urgently as he ran, clutching two rifles.

Darrow's eyes expressed doubt for a moment, then he dismissed them from his thoughts, turning to his deputies. He gestured them to windows either side of the door. Pacey grabbed the table where the euchre players had been a few moments before, and tipped it over in a shower of cards and coins. Hugh followed his example at the other window, glad of the shelter as he checked the rounds in his Webley. He glanced up in time to see Tomcat reach the other side of the street and swarm up the front of the general store. For a moment, he forgot his fear as he watched Tomcat's effortless, gravity-defying climb. Within seconds, Tomcat was over the false front of the store building, and on to the flat roof. Below, Irish reached the side of the building. He tossed a rifle up to Tomcat, then took shelter behind a stack of barrels. Only then did Hugh realize he could hear horses pounding along the street and getting closer, fast.

Croucher and his three men swept into view, all holding pistols. They spied the lawmen's horses tied outside the saloon, and turned towards them.

'Darrow! Come out, you yellow-gutted lawdog!' Croucher yelled.

The saloon door was only open about a foot; Darrow shouted back through the gap.

'Surrender! You're surrounded!'

Croucher turned his horse to the saloon door and fired a fast shot by way of answer.

Gunfire erupted all around. Hugh hastily ducked behind the upturned table, hunching down as broken glass showered over his hat and shoulders. He shook himself, spraying glass shards, and took a deep breath. Lunging to his feet, he fired two fast shots at the riders on the other side of the shattered window. Just before Gemmill fired back, turning more glass into fragments, Hugh heard Tomcat calling a challenge from across the street. One of the two men facing Hugh, Fenner, wrenched his horse's head round and raked his spurs along its side. The bay mare flattened her ears and buck-jumped forwards, spoiling Fenner's attempt to draw his second pistol.

Darrow was using the partly-open saloon door as cover, exchanging shots with Croucher. Just beyond them, Johnson was facing Pacey, and being fired on from above by Whiskers and Donnington, who were leaning out of a first floor window. Hugh felt something trickling down his neck, inside his collar, but didn't know if it was blood or sweat. He fired again and saw Gemmill rock in his saddle. For a moment there was the elation of hitting his target, but it was quickly swamped by the familiar sick feeling that came from knowing he'd deliberately injured another living being. The big man was struggling to raise his Colt and aim it at Hugh. Peering from behind the overturned table, Hugh yelled an order for the outlaw to surrender.

Fenner was under fire from both Tomcat and Irish. Cursing his horse and Tomcat equally, he managed to draw his second pistol while firing wildly at Irish with the first. A bullet from Tomcat's rifle scored across the top of his left shoulder.

'Goddam you!' Fenner shrieked.

Firing both pistols at once, Fenner jammed his spurs into his horse's sides. The mare reared in protest, forcing Fenner to grab for her mane as she went vertical. A shot from Tomcat hit him in the shoulder. Fenner jerked back, and the shift in his weight pulled the horse over. Dropping both guns and kicking his feet free of the stirrups, Fenner tried to jump clear as the horse crashed down on top of him. He was too slow. His shriek of fear was abruptly cut off as the high pommel of the saddle was driven into his chest by half a ton of horse falling across his torso. The mare rolled on him as she struggled back to her feet, crushing him. Frothy blood bubbled briefly from his nose and mouth as Fenner died on the dirt street.

Johnson also fell; under fire from Pacey, Whiskers and Donnington, he had no chance. He slid from his saddle, dropping his pistol, and lay moaning.

Croucher fired at Darrow, but the sheriff was sheltering behind the sturdy door of the saloon. The amount of gunfire all around told Croucher that his men were outnumbered but he didn't look to see what was happening. Darrow had killed his brother, and now Darrow had trapped him. This was his last chance to kill the man who had ruined everything. With a roar of fury, Tom Croucher urged his horse forward and the bay mare obediently leapt towards the saloon door.

There was no point in closing the door. Darrow had no means to bar it, and the catch wouldn't hold if a horse crashed into it. Instead, Darrow pulled the door wide open as Croucher's horse leaped on to the low sidewalk. He moved to his right, forcing Croucher to change aim in order to shoot along the other side of his horse's neck. Croucher still fired first, as Darrow had expected. The sheriff spent a fraction longer in aiming, gambling that Croucher's hasty shot from a moving horse would miss, even at this close range. Splinters kicked out from the door frame where Croucher's bullet hit. As Croucher cocked his pistol for a second shot, Darrow fired.

His shot tore into Croucher's chest, rocking him back in his saddle. His horse propped to a sharp halt, further swaying him.

'Damn you, Darrow!'

Croucher stayed in his saddle, but his shot went wild. Darrow barely shifted, coolly changing his aim just slightly. His bullet took Croucher in the head. The outlaw buckled, falling limply across his horse's rump, then sliding sideways. His boot caught in the stirrup and his body dangled from the saddle as his horse snorted and spun. Poised ready with his pistol cocked, Darrow glanced about. Jackson was on the ground, as was the crushed corpse of Fenner. Gemmill was still in his saddle, but had dropped his gun and raised his one good arm in a gesture of surrender.

Catching the bay mare's reins, Darrow calmed her. He holstered his Colt and moved round to Croucher's body. Slowly, the sheriff removed the pocket watch and chain that Croucher wore, and looked at them. He stayed still as the others came out and began dealing with the aftermath of the gunfight, his eyes fixed on the watch. With a sudden movement, he thrust the watch and chain into his jacket pocket and returned his attention to his surroundings.

Hugh was out on the sidewalk and had been watching him. He raised an eyebrow in silent enquiry and Darrow nodded, a sudden smile transforming his face.

'Oh, good,' Hugh said. 'Can we go home now?'

* ★ *

Tomcat and Irish applauded as Hugh completed the magic trick.

'For sure, those tricks of yours are good,' Irish said.

Hugh bowed, and leaned back against the desk of the law office in Govan.

'I surely do wish you'd teach me some tricks,' Tomcat pleaded. 'I'm going straight now. I gotta find ways of earning money, instead of stealing it.'

Hugh considered, as he shuffled the deck of cards he'd been using. He was saved from having to answer by Baldwin, who arrived clutching a brown envelope.

'Telegram for the sheriff,' Baldwin

announced, putting the envelope on the leather-topped desk.

Hugh picked it up and opened it.

'That's for Sheriff Darrow!' Baldwin protested.

'Darrow's not here,' Hugh replied, reading the message. 'He's in that council meeting, remember? This could be something urgent, and just think how angry he'd be if it was, and nothing got done because we'd waited.'

'You're just nosy,' Tomcat remarked.

'That too,' Hugh acknowledged, unperturbed. 'It's from Pacey. Gemmill is strong enough to travel, so they're coming back on the stage, leaving Holt tomorrow.'

Pacey had stayed behind with the wounded outlaw, who had been unfit to ride back with the others. The delay until the weekly stagecoach ran through Holt to Govan gave Gemmill some time to recover before making the two-day journey.

'I guess he'll be going in one of the single cells,' Baldwin said to Hugh. 'If he's injured, it could be a long whiles before he comes to trial, and that's less space to fit in our regular number of lawbreakers.'

'That won't be a problem by next year.' Darrow was just inside the doorway. He strolled forward, to join the group around the desk. 'Marshal Pacey will have more room for his drunks and petty criminals.'

Hugh caught the implication first. 'The council agreed to your proposals? The town gets a marshal and we get to concentrate on doing county law work?'

Darrow smiled. 'I showed them the figures — the number of arrests we make each week, and the numbers given jail terms. I made out what a shame it was we had to rely on Laramie to look after our prisoners. They got to thinking it was a matter of civic pride that Govan should have its own jail. I also reminded them that it would bring money into the town, what with needing supplies,' he added.

Hugh laughed. 'I bet half the

councillors were drafting their bids for contracts before the meeting finished.'

'So who's going to be working where?' Baldwin asked, scratching his leg.

'You'll stay a deputy sheriff and work with me and Hugh,' Darrow answered. 'That empty store next to the photographer's at the north end of Main Street will be the sheriff's main office. The county jail will be built on the far side of the river. Pacey will be based here, as town marshal.' He paused, and looked at Tomcat and Irish. 'He'll need at least two deputies.'

Tomcat started to reply, then paused and looked at his friend. Irish smiled and spoke.

'Surely we're after being grateful for the offer, but I don't think we'll be taking it.'

'It's not so long since we got out of that jail,' Tomcat said. 'I don't want to be tying myself to one place, not for a whiles, anyhow.'

'What are you going to do?' asked Baldwin.

Tomcat shrugged. 'Try herding cattle, maybe.'

'Oh! I know!' Hugh exclaimed. He dug around in the pockets of his jacket, and produced coins, string, a penknife and a cigarette card with a picture of an actress, before finding an envelope of high quality paper, with British stamps.

'Richard wrote to me the other week,' he said, extracting the letter. 'You remember my brother, don't you?' he asked Tomcat and Irish.

'I sure do.' Tomcat absently rubbed the back of his head.

'Richard wrote that Harry Faulkner-Greene is coming over here in a month or so,' Hugh went on.

'Harry Faulkner-Greene? That's a whole mouthful of a name,' Tomcat said.

Hugh looked up and grinned. 'He's Lord Henry Faulkner-Greene, Viscount of Attleborough, in full. Anyway, he's coming over, to Colorado, to do some hunting. Richard wants me to find a guide for him, someone who can show him some good sport, arrange for suitable horses and kit out an expedition into the mountains, that kind of thing. He'll pay well — he can damn well afford to — and I'm willing to recommend you two, if you'd like the job.'

Irish and Tomcat grinned at one another.

'Escort a real English nob out on a hunting trip?' Irish said. 'For sure and I never thought I'd be rubbing shoulders with a for-real lord.'

'How long's he gonna be here?' Tomcat asked.

Hugh glanced at the letter again. 'Richard thinks it'll be about six weeks.'

Irish shrugged. 'That ain't long, so it don't matter too much iffen we don't like him.'

'Reckon as we'll give it a whirl then,' Tomcat said, grinning.

'Now you've got that sorted, it's time Hugh went out on the rounds,' Darrow ordered.

Hugh sighed, then stuffed the letter back into the envelope and returned it with the other odds and ends to his pockets. Picking up his shotgun, he promised Tomcat and Irish that he'd write to his brother that evening, and headed out. Somewhat to his surprise, Darrow also left, strolling along the sidewalk in the same direction. When Hugh looked at him curiously, the sheriff explained that he was going along to look at the empty building that would be their new office.

'It'll be strange, not doing the rounds, once the marshal's office takes over the town work,' Hugh mused, hurrying slightly to avoid a dray turning into Cross Street.

Darrow slowed, and turned to look at him for a few moments.

'You could work for the marshal's office, if you prefer,' he said. 'You'd spend more time in town, and wouldn't have to be away from Minnie and the baby.'

Hugh shook his head. 'I don't want Pacey as my boss. He'd bully me and get angry at me.'

Darrow gave him a curious look. 'I bully you and get angry at you.'

'I know. But you're also willing to bend the rules, and you care too much about your own skin to rush stupidly into danger and drag me along. Even when you take a gamble, as you did in freeing Irish and Tomcat, you assess the risk first.'

'I am flattered by your shrewd judgement of my character,' Darrow drawled.

Hugh nodded. 'You're welcome. And in any case, I always believe in the phrase 'better the devil you know'.'

Darrow declined to answer that.

THE END